"Catherine, a... some..."

She blinked, startled. "What? For heaven's sake. No. Of course not."

Jason observed her carefully. "Then what's with the nursery? That's a lot of work to go through for nothing. I know you mentioned wanting to become a mother. Maybe you're planning on adopting?"

Catherine twirled her hair. "Not exactly." She took a deep breath. "Funny you should bring this up, Jason, because I've been meaning to ask you something."

His eyes never left her face. "What?"

She sipped her coffee and studied the inside of the mug as though it held the secret of life. Finally she blurted out what she'd been holding inside all these weeks. "Jason, would you consider giving me a baby?"

Dear Reader,

To ring in 1998—Romance-style!—we've got some new voices and some exciting new love stories from the authors you love.

Valerie Parv is best known for her Harlequin Romance and Presents novels, but *The Billionaire's Baby Chase*, this month's compelling FABULOUS FATHERS title, marks her commanding return to Silhouette! This billionaire daddy is *pure* alpha male...and no one—not even the heroine!—will keep him from his long-lost daughter....

Doreen Roberts's sparkling new title, *In Love with the Boss*, features the classic boss/secretary theme. Discover how a no-nonsense temp catches the eye—and heart—of her wealthy brooding boss. If you want to laugh out loud, don't miss Terry Essig's *What the Nursery Needs...* In this charming story, what the *heroine* needs is the right man to make a baby! Hmm...

A disillusioned rancher finds himself thinking, *Say You'll Stay and Marry Me*, when he falls for the beautiful wanderer who is stranded on his ranch in this emotional tale by Patti Standard. And, believe me, if you think *The Bride, the Trucker and the Great Escape* sounds fun, just wait till you read this engaging romantic adventure by Suzanne McMinn. And in *The Sheriff with the Wyoming-Size Heart* by Kathy Jacobson, emotions run high as a small-town lawman and a woman with secrets try to give romance a chance....

And there's *much* more to come in 1998! I hope you enjoy our selections this month—and every month.

Happy New Year!

Joan Marlow Golan
Senior Editor
Silhouette Books

Please address questions and book requests to:
Silhouette Reader Service
U.S.: 3010 Walden Ave., P.O. Box 1325, Buffalo, NY 14269
Canadian: P.O. Box 609, Fort Erie, Ont. L2A 5X3

WHAT THE NURSERY NEEDS...

Terry Essig

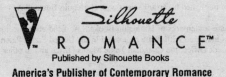

Silhouette

R O M A N C E™

Published by Silhouette Books

America's Publisher of Contemporary Romance

To Stephanie Scharf,
for all those long drives to Chicago's Inner City
to help me teach art. And to her husband, David Taber,
for his help and support.
You're both the best.

 SILHOUETTE BOOKS

ISBN 0-373-19272-X

WHAT THE NURSERY NEEDS…

Copyright © 1998 by Terry Parent Essig

Printed in U.S.A.

Books by Terry Essig

Silhouette Romance

House Calls #552
The Wedding March #662
Fearless Father #725
Housemates #1015
Hardheaded Woman #1044
Daddy on Board #1114
Mad for the Dad #1198
What the Nursery Needs... #1272

Silhouette Special Edition

Father of the Brood #796

TERRY ESSIG

lives in northern Indiana. She has six children, a wonderful husband and a crazy English setter. (Better the dog than the husband, although with all the music lessons, sport activities and general mayhem, the husband may more than occasionally feel like he's losing his mind.) Terry finds it all, uh, good inspiration for her writing?

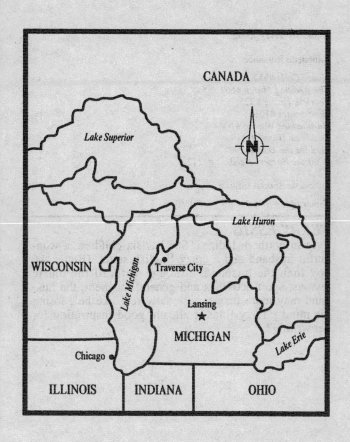

Chapter One

The dark blue sedan drew up to the curb, its speed slowing to match the pace of the young preadolescent girl walking down the sidewalk. With a near silent whisper, the passenger side window slid down. The driver leaned over to call out through the opening, "Hey, you with the snazzy earrings, want a ride? I've got candy." He let the temptation dangle in the air between them.

The child, temporarily forgetting the embarrassment of her barely burgeoning breasts, pulled her shoulders back and glared in the direction of the car. "No, thanks," she said, adjusting her backpack strap on her shoulder and picking up her pace. "My *father* doesn't want me talking to strange men."

The man behind the wheel slumped briefly. The emphasis on the word *father* didn't bode well. Whatever happened to *daddy?* He sighed and stepped slightly on the gas. The car surged just enough to keep him abreast of the girl. "Oh, come on. Don't be like that. I've got a ton of candy in here. Wouldn't you like a treat after a hard day at school?"

The girl stopped in her tracks and turned to face the car. "What kind of candy?" she asked.

"Get in the car and I'll show you."

"It's probably something I don't even like."

"Bet it's not. I bet it's your favorite."

At that, the girl flipped her ponytail and left the safety of the sidewalk. She approached the car. "Oh, yeah? Let's see." Her eyes widened at the variety of candy bars displayed on the front seat. Without hesitating any further, she opened the passenger door and slid in. The car gunned away from the curb to merge seemlessly back into traffic.

Her favorite was indeed there, but when the girl made to take it, the man's hand stayed hers. "The deal is if you take that, it means the snit is officially over and you have to start talking to me again."

The preadolescent's eyes narrowed as she considered the catch. "Will you let Connie and me go to the mall together?"

"No. Not without an adult. My answer to that won't change. I work with somebody whose name is forever sealed behind my lips, so don't ask, whose niece runs in that same group. She tells me Connie and another girl were picked up for shoplifting some makeup—lipstick and stuff like that. The manager of the store let it drop when Connie's mother made her apologize and pay double, but she might not be so lucky next time. If you're out with somebody like that, even if you haven't taken anything yourself, you could get picked up as an accessory, to say nothing of the fact that it just isn't safe for two young girls to be at the mall by themselves. And don't start on how nothing ever happens in South Bend or even the entire state of Indiana. You've said it all before and I still say there are too many weirdos out there.''

"Connie said she didn't know how that lipstick got in her pocket. She thinks maybe it rolled off the shelf while she was standing there. Or else maybe Angie slipped it into her shorts pocket at the checkout when she was waiting to pay for her gum, just to get her in trouble. They had a fight that day.''

The disbelieving adult snort was loud and prolonged. "Yeah, right. How stupid do I look?''

"Besides, lots of other kids I know have tried shoplifting. They just didn't get caught.''

"Let me put it to you this way, sweetie. You even *think* about trying it and you won't set so much as a big toe outside your bedroom door for a month of Sundays. Understand?''

"But, Dad…''

Jason John Engel silently ground his teeth at his daughter's whining tone. "I mean it, Maura, issues like this are nonnegotiable. The candy doesn't mean I'm weakening, just that I'm willing to sweeten the refusal. Like I told you before, I can probably take you and a friend, preferably not Connie, to the mall this weekend, if you want.''

"No. Everybody else gets to go to the mall by themselves. It would be too embarrassing if anybody saw. I'd never be able to face my friends again.''

Jason shrugged, knowing he shouldn't take her rejection personally, but doing so, anyway. "Fine. Then you don't go.''

His twelve-year-old daughter, he noticed, ground her teeth exactly the way he did when frustrated. But she did take the candy bar. He waited until after her first bite. "So we're talking again, right?"

Maura's mouth stilled briefly as she stopped chewing and eyed him. Jason just hoped she wasn't going to spit the candy all over him. He was wearing a good suit. Eventually she nodded her head in the affirmative.

Jason was afraid his relief was palpable in the car. It was scary how much control a twelve-year-old could wield with her moods and whims. It amounted to emotional blackmail at times.

"By the way," he said. "I want you to walk home from school on the opposite side of the street from now on. Did you see how easy it was for me to stay next to you and talk to you? If I'd have had a mind to, I could have easily hopped out of the car and grabbed you. On the other side of the street, you'd be walking against traffic, and it would be much harder for anybody in a car to harrass you."

"Dad," Maura began kindly, too kindly for Jason's peace of mind. In his experience, that kind of patient tone boded nothing but ill for what followed.

"Maura, please, let's not argue about this, too. Just do it, all right? Just do it."

"Okay, fine, whatever."

"Thank you," Jason said fervently and meant it. He was so grateful, he pretended not to notice the heavy-duty eye rolling that accompanied the exasperated agreement. "Thank you very much." He pulled around a corner onto his own street, and three blocks later pulled into his driveway.

Maura leaned forward interestedly as the car stopped next to the house. "Look, Dad, there's somebody moving in next door."

"Hmm?" Jason glanced up from collecting his briefcase and newspaper to see what had caught his daughter's attention. "Oh, that's nice. That house has been empty for so long I didn't think anybody would ever buy it. Vacant houses lower the property values in an area. And, I suppose it'll be good to have neighbors again, eh, Maura?"

"I wonder if there's anybody my age."

"Could be," her father mumbled noncommittally as he fumbled with the door handle. "We'll have to wait and see."

Maura's shoulders slumped more than usual as she walked around the rear of the car. "Look, they're moving in a crib and a bassinet. I guess that means no friend for me."

"Not necessarily," Jason said as he pushed his key into the front door lock. "The baby could have an older sister and if not, think about the baby-sitting jobs that could come your way." Money always appealed at this age. The thought of it should perk Maura right up.

It did, too. Her shoulders briefly straightened before she remembered to round them again. "Yes, Annie O'Connor had the cutest sweatshirt on at school yesterday, but she said it cost $38 and I knew you'd never pay that much for a sweatshirt. If I earn half baby-sitting, do you think you'd pay the other half, Dad?"

Jason set his briefcase down on the wooden floor of the front foyer and balanced his newspaper on top of it before tiredly rubbing his eye. "Uh, I'll think about it, okay? Don't eat any more of those candy bars before dinner, Maura," he instructed as he noticed the fistful she clasped. "I don't want you filling up on junk. Do me a favor and ration them over the next few days so I don't feel so guilty about buying you such swill."

Maura shrugged and crossed her fingers behind her back. "Okay, no problem, Dad."

"Terrific," Jason said, not believing a word of it. "I'm going to change, then see what I can put together for dinner. You're in charge of a salad."

"No prob."

Jason merely grunted on his way up the stairs. Man, what a day. But at least Maura was more or less speaking to him again—if you could call this communicating.

Next door, Catherine Marie Nicholson let out a grunt. "There," she said as she hefted another heavy cardboard box onto a stack of similar boxes in her new kitchen. "That's the last of the dish boxes I think. Next time I move, I'm going to remember not to put so much in the boxes. These suckers are heavy!"

"Next time you move," her sister Monica responded as she leaned against the countertops while she caught her breath, "you'll have to give me more of an advance notice so I can be sure to have other plans for the day."

"You don't mean that," Catherine assured her as she filled two cups with tap water and handed one to Monica.

"Oh, yes I do."

"I'll make it up to you. How about if I take Amy all day Saturday? You can spend it pottering around doing whatever you feel like."

Monica set her cup down after chugging the liquid. "What kind of deal is that? You adore Amy. You're always trying to get your grimy little mitts on her so that you can have your monthly 'kid fix.' When are you going to break down and have one of your own?"

"Actually, I've been giving that a great deal of thought lately," Catherine admitted to her sister.

"Yeah? Come to any earth-shattering conclusions? Like time to stop being so darn picky and marry Gerald?"

"Don't be ridiculous." Catherine made a dismissing gesture. "I'll never be that hard up. Gerald and I had already been out looking for a diamond when I discovered he was seeing Caroline Neeley on the sly. That poor girl had no idea Gerald had proposed to me, the dirtbag. No, forget Gerald. Forget men. I've come up with a different approach entirely." She reached for the cleaning supplies she'd stacked in one corner. "Help me wipe out the cabinets and lay some shelf paper so I can start emptying these boxes, will you?"

"Having a baby is not exactly a do-it-yourself kind of project, you know. You're a natural nurturer. It's why you keep borrowing Amy. It's why you keep falling in love with the cribs you sell in your kids' resale shop. You need children of your own to feel fulfilled. You know that and I know that. You've been looking for Mr. Right for close to five years now," Monica said as she grudgingly picked up a sponge.

"Why give up now? Twenty-seven isn't that old. You've still got time."

"Nope. Gerald was the last straw. I give up. I'm throwing in the towel. I decided just last night, as a matter of fact, that it was time to move on to plan B."

"I didn't know there was a plan B."

"There wasn't. Now there is. It's simple. Go to a sperm bank."

Monica almost fell off the ladder she was standing on. "What?"

"You heard me. Cut out the middle man, go directly to the source. From what I understand, people do it all the time."

Catherine dunked her sponge in her bucket and began to wipe out the interior of a bottom cabinet. Her plan made perfect sense to her. One had to be flexible in this life. A determined person could always find a way to achieve her goal.

Monica, however, was not convinced. "That doesn't make any sense at all. You'd be adding a middle man, not taking one away. The man *is* the source."

Catherine pulled her head out of the cabinet she'd been scrubbing and threw her sponge into the bucket, splashing soapsuds on the floor. "Fine, if you want to play word games, be that way, but you know what I mean. If I really want a baby, which I do, I need to start rethinking the whole project. Otherwise it's going to remain nothing but an unattainable dream." She squeezed out the sponge and attacked the next cabinet in line.

Monica opened the cabinet next to the one she'd

just finished. Her voice was muffled now and echoed slightly, but her disapproval was still clear. "You were always daydreaming and playing pretend as a kid. You've gotten a lot better about getting real. We're all so proud of the way you've made your business succeed, but there's such a thing as taking it too far. Just be patient. Some guy will turn up, and I'd hate to have you miss all the fun involved in creating a baby naturally. I meant what I said about you being a natural candidate for motherhood, Cath, but I know you like I know the back of my own hand, and I'm telling you I don't think you'll be happy doing it this way. You crave family. The whole shebang. You need the husband to go along with the kiddies. I know."

"Yes, well, unfortunately, Prince Charming is taken, Monica. Cinderella got her claws into him before I even had a chance. I almost made a very bad mistake out of what I now see was desperation. I'm not going to risk it again."

Monica sat heavily on the third step of her ladder. "But a *sperm bank?* It seems so cold—so impersonal. Your baby's not going to know its daddy?" she asked weakly.

Catherine backed out of the cabinet and shrugged at her sister. "Desperate times call for desperate measures. A lady brought in the most beautiful four-poster canopy crib for me to sell for her last week. I brought it home. As a matter of fact, last night I also decided to decorate the spare bedroom as a nursery instead of an office. What do you think of that?"

"Oh, my God, you're really serious about this."

Catherine nodded emphatically. "You bet I am. I'm going to decorate that room, set up the crib, then fill it. I am not about to go sit in there every evening and get maudlin over the empty crib. I've got my college degree, my resale shop is doing fantastically well, and now I've even got my own home. Things aren't going to get much more orderly than that, and so I'm going to bite the bullet. No time like the present, and all of that. I'm going for it, Mon."

Monica stared at her sister. "I can't believe this."

Catherine nodded firmly. "Believe it."

"Do you even know where there is a sperm bank?"

"No, but how difficult can they be to find? You read about people using them all the time in the newspaper."

"Usually because there's been a problem. All the sperm defrosted or somebody's is missing. Something awful like that."

Catherine shrugged off Monica's concern. "Well, they're not going to publish the normal day-to-day success cases, are they? You know the press. They only publish the grimmest of the grim."

"I don't know, Cath. I mean, what if you got over-fertilized and ended up with sextuplets or something? I hear that happens all the time at those places. How would you handle a multiple birth all by yourself? You'd be too tired to run the shop.

"And besides, I bet you don't have even the fog-giest idea how to find a sperm bank or what to do or say if you did. Do you know anybody who knows anything about this? Outside of the newspaper stories, I mean. Those all seemed to be in California, as I recall, and you don't want a baby born with a need to go surfing. He'd be in for a real disappointment here in South Bend.''

''All right, so I'll rule out any sperm that might have originated in California,'' Catherine agreed with a shrug. ''It's a big country, even without California. I'm sure there are plenty of other sperm out there. And think about this, Mon. Doing it this way I can have the absolute baby of my dreams. I can probably just give them a checklist of attributes I want. Blond hair, blue eyes, IQ over 120.''

Monica rolled her eyes, and Catherine gave her a disapproving look.

''Quit being so discouraging. I'm telling you, my plan is scientifically sound. I'd have a say in all that stuff, whereas if I sit around waiting to fall in love, I'd have to take whatever I've fallen for. Gerald wasn't all that hot looking, but he was smart and seemed nice enough—or so I thought. This way, I can have it all. Oops, we'll have to finish talking about this later. Here comes dinner.''

And in fact, before Catherine could even pull herself to her feet, the back door opened to admit Monica's husband and their twelve-year-old daughter, both carrying bags brimming over with small white cartons of Chinese takeout.

''We're back,'' Don Davies announced as though a broad-shouldered six-foot-two man stood a chance of going unnoticed. ''And we've got supper with us. You two find the plates and silverware yet?''

''We're not quite ready,'' Catherine said as she emptied her bucket into the sink. ''We got kind of distracted,'' she confessed with a glare at her sister. ''But I know what box they're in.'' Catherine had known Donald a long time. The man got cranky when he got hungry. It was best to keep him fed. "Everything go okay?" she asked as she began to rearrange boxes to get at what she hoped was the right one.

"Yep," Don assured her as he began pulling cartons from the bags and setting them on the kitchen table. "This smells good. I'm starving. We returned the rented van—you owe me an extra twenty-seven bucks, by the way—dropped off John, picked up the food and came right back. Todd and Mary Fran take off?" he asked, naming several more relatives who had helped with the move.

"Yes," Monica confirmed before Catherine had a chance. "Just a little while ago."

Don moved all the boxes and papers that had been stacked all over the table and onto the countertop. "There, now we've got some room. You find those forks yet?"

"I think so—yes! Here they are." Catherine looked up from the carton she'd just pulled the flap up from to successfully wave an eating implement.

There was an unexpected knock and all four heads turned to glance curiously at the back door.

"You expecting anybody?" Don asked Catherine, immediately slipping into the role of protective brother-in-law.

Catherine shook her head.

"Well," Monica huffed, but at least she kept her voice down, "you'd think the neighbors would at least give you a day or two to unpack before they descend on you."

"Amy, honey, would you get that for me?" Catherine asked. "I've still got to find the box with the dinner plates."

A few moments later Amy returned with a girl about her age. "Aunt Cath," Amy said, drawing the girl into the room, "this is my friend from school, Maura. Guess what?"

"What?"

"Maura lives right next door to you."

Catherine said, "Awesome. You can see each other when you're over, Amy."

Amy nodded wisely. "I know."

"And maybe sometimes when I borrow you from your mom so we can go out and do girl stuff, Maura's mom will let me borrow her, too, and all three of us can go. What do you think?"

"Cool. Isn't that the best, Maura?" Amy asked.

"Oh, I hardly ever see my mom," Maura informed Catherine. "She sends me cards and stuff, but she's too busy with her new family in Chicago and can't get away to see me too much anymore. But I could ask my dad." Maura, who'd been looking quite pleased and eager over this new development in her life, appeared suddenly doubtful. "Maybe he'd let me."

Catherine smiled, briefly flashing her dimples. "It can't hurt to ask, right?" she said to her new neighbor. But she couldn't help wondering what kind of father wouldn't let a child go out on a well-chaperoned excursion to such a nearby and unexotic destination as the local mall. "Amy, has Maura met your mom and dad? Maybe you'd better introduce them."

Maura turned to beam a smile at Monica and Don.

"Hi, Mr. and Mrs. Davies, remember me? I met you at the girls' basketball game the other night."

Before Monica or Don had a chance to respond, there was another knock on the door.

Don eyed the cartons of takeout in long-suffering martyrdom. "Good grief, this is turning into Grand Central Station. We're never going to get to eat." He groaned as Monica gave him an elbow in the ribs and a warning frown.

Catherine opened the back door to find a large and rather handsome, albeit frantic-looking, male on her back patio.

"Excuse me," the stranger began before Catherine could get out a single word, "I live right next door," and he pointed right next door to illustrate his claim. "My daughter seems to be missing, and I was wondering if by any remote possibility—Maura, there you are. My God, child, you almost put me into an early grave. Don't ever just take off like that again, do you hear me?"

Catherine looked over her shoulder to see how Maura was taking this parental outburst. The child wore a long-suffering expression that made Catherine smile.

"Daaad," his progeny moaned in despair. "What did you think, that I got kidnapped or something? I was making a salad like you said for me to do. I looked out the window and saw my friend Amy. I ran over to see if this was her new house, but it's not. I'm just saying hello, and I'll be back in a couple of minutes to finish the salad, okay?"

Jason took a calming breath, wondering as he did so if he would live through his daughter's preadolescence. You could forget the actual teenage years. There was no doubt in his mind he'd be six feet under long before he managed to shepherd her through adolescence, but he would like to eke out another year or two of life before his heart gave up in disgust. "Maura, it wouldn't have even taken two seconds for you to yell up the stairs and tell me what you were doing. Two seconds."

"It's not like I knew you were going to blow a gasket or anything."

"Honey, I thought you were still mad at me and had taken off again. It took me three hours to find you after I yelled at you for the cigarette pack I found in your room."

"Well, that wasn't fair because I was just keeping it for Marissa. She didn't want her mother to find it at her house."

Jason arched a brow. "The only reason I even thought to look through your things was because some of your clothing smelled like smoke when I was doing the laundry."

"Oh. Well—"

"Don't bother. The point is I'd made it halfway through the student directory before Kelsey Earling's mother admitted you were there. I wasn't looking forward to going through that again."

Jason took a deep breath to settle himself. "Okay. You didn't run away. You have my apology for thinking such evil thoughts. Now, since you've already barged in on the new neighbors, why don't you introduce me?"

"Cath," Don practically barked, "the plates?"

"For heaven's sake, Donald," Catherine replied

tersely. "I found you a fork, didn't I? Just eat it out of the darn carton and keep quiet."

Great, thought Jason tiredly. As if he didn't have enough of it, the new neighbors were the kind who sniped at each other. How wonderful. Patiently he stuck the introductions out. "I understand your husband's irritation. You've had a long day with the moving and all. And we're interrupting your dinner. My name is Jason Engel, that's my daughter, Maura, and we are leaving—right now. Maura, say goodbye to your friend. Welcome to the neighborhood. Nice to meet you all. Come on, kiddo, you've got a salad to finish up."

Maura immediately dug in her heels. "But, Dad..."

After a year of raising his daughter all by himself, Jason was finally beginning to understand the necessity of heading this kind of thing off at the pass, child-rearing books be damned. "No ands, ifs, or buts about it, sweetie, we're going. This falls under the general heading of rudeness and learning how not to be."

Catherine was enjoying Maura's antics. As for Jason Engel, well, he seemed frazzled, but all right in his own way. His heart seemed in the right place, at any rate. If she wanted to get to know the daughter better, maybe borrow her if she needed a kid fix and Amy was busy, Catherine knew instinctively she'd have to walk a fine line with the father and avoid alienating him. She could tell he was very protective of his offspring.

"If it's any consolation," Monica said to Jason, "your daughter waited a year longer than Amy here before trying a cigarette. Fortunately, it made her as sick as a dog and that was the end of that."

"Mom," Amy wailed with a horrified look. "How did you know?"

"You think I didn't know what was behind your green complexion and upset stomach when you came home from that overnight last fall? With the way your clothing reeked of tobacco? Get real, kid. I wasn't born yesterday." Monica looked Jason Engel up and down speculatively. "I've got an idea," she said. You could almost see the proverbial lightbulb flash over her head. "Don bought enough Chinese for one of my brothers and his wife, too, but they had to leave. Why don't you and Maura finish up your salad and bring it over here? By the time you get back, Catherine or I will have found the plates and we'll all share what we've got."

Maura looked pleadingly at her father, and he knew if he said no, he'd be out buying more candy bars tomorrow. Oh, well. "Maura, it's infringing. They haven't even had a chance to open a box yet—"

"They could all come to our house, couldn't they, Dad? That wouldn't be infringing. It would be gracious on our part, right?"

Catherine had to hide a grin at the child's ingenuousness. She turned her attention back to Jason and waited.

"Ordinarily, you'd be right," Jason replied. "But as you well know, there are exceptions to every rule. Times when normal protocol doesn't apply."

Maura scowled suspiciously. "Like when?"

"Like when somebody gets so excited at seeing somebody they know, they race out of the house without turning off the kitchen faucet."

Maura studied the floor. "Oh. But nothing bad happ—"

"Like when the lettuce that somebody was washing covers up the drain in that sink, causing it to overflow."

"Uh-oh."

"And finally, like when that same somebody's father races into the kitchen to get to the tap, slides on the wet floor, tries to catch himself only to knock a bottle of salad dressing off the countertop and have it smash all over the floor leaving glass shards everywhere that he hasn't had time to clean up yet because he went looking for his daughter. That's like when."

Maura looked everywhere but at her father. She cleared her throat. "Yes, well, sorry about that, Dad."

Catherine finally took pity. "Sounds like you've had a heck of an afternoon," she told Jason. "Let the mess sit there for a while. It won't go anywhere. As long as you don't object to the chaos here, I don't mind. Sit down. Eat. Fortify yourself for the cleanup ahead of you."

Maura looked at her father pleadingly.

Jason rubbed the back of his neck in a tired gesture. "All right, if you're sure you don't mind. I'll go salvage what I can of the salad. I think I've got another bottle of salad dressing in the fridge. Maura, you come help."

Maura grabbed Amy's hand and tugged her along in her wake. "Amy can come too, right, Dad?"

Jason grunted his agreement as he opened the back door and held it for the two girls. They shot through the opening and kept right on going. He sighed. "When a gentleman holds the door for you, you're supposed to say 'thank you,'" he called after them, shaking his head. Damn, but this parenting was *work*.

"I don't have any beer in the house," Catherine

advised him. "I'm afraid you'll have to bring your own if you don't want pop or water."

Jason shook his head regretfully. He could sure use one. "I don't keep anything alcoholic in the house," he said with a sigh of regret. Not since Karen had remarried and Maura had come to live with him. Bad example. "Water or soda will be fine. We'll be back in five minutes, no more, I promise."

As soon as the door slammed, Monica was up and standing on tiptoes to look out the kitchen window at their retreating backs. "Did you hear what that little girl said, Cath?"

"No, what?"

Monica grabbed both Catherine's arms and held her still. She spoke softly, not wanting Don to overhear. "Cath, that child said it was just her and her dad living there. The mother's remarried."

"Yes, so?"

"So, he's tall and has a nice body to go along with the height. If his hair was any darker brown it would be black, eyes to match. He's as handsome as sin. Good God, the man even has manners. Forget about your blond, blue-eyes fetish for a minute. Did you see the way he held the door for the girls? My gosh, if I can see it, why can't you? That, my dear, is prime marital material! I'm thinking that you can still have it all! Why, any idiot with even minimal level hormones could fall for that hunk. All you would have to do is get him to fall in love with *you,* and presto, instant family."

Chapter Two

Catherine couldn't keep her jaw from dropping open. "I can only hope," she whispered to her sister, "that whatever form of madness you have suddenly developed is not genetic in nature. I find you downright frightening at times—especially since we're related."

With a flick of her hand, Monica brushed Catherine's insult off. "Let's think about this with an open mind, sister, dear. The man was tall, he was dark, he was handsome. He conveniently lives right next door. In my opinion you could make beautiful babies together."

"You are insane. We've barely met the man and you're already marrying me off to him?"

"What are you two whispering about over there? Would you kill me if we started without them, Monica? I'm half-dead from hunger," Don grumped.

"We're talking about what a grouch you are when you're hungry, Don."

Don managed a wounded look. "I'm a paragon, a saint, I tell you. I put up with the two of you, don't I?"

Monica turned her back on her husband and resumed her lecture. "Think about the embarrassment factor of doing it your way, Cath. Even if we manage to locate one of those sperm bank places, you're going to have to walk in and explain what you want. Think about that, sweetie pie."

Catherine did, flushed and swallowed hard. "Oh, well, when you put it that way I can see that this idea of yours makes perfect sense. Just tell me one thing.

"What's that?"

"If I'm not brave enough to march into a sperm bank and explain what I want, and let's face it, they'd have to at least have a suspicion of what's on my mind—only carrying one product the way they do—what makes you think I'll be able to propose marriage and parenthood to Jason Engel?"

Monica sighed and closed her eyes. "Nobody's asking you to propose tonight, Cath. Patience is its own reward, remember that. You'll be living right next door to the man. All you have to do is make sure you spend some time together every now and again over the next little while, so that any little seeds we plant get a chance to bear fruit."

"They're here," Don announced, as a brief knock sounded on the back door before the handle turned.

"We're back," Amy announced, running into the room. "The water's mopped up and the glass is gone, but the floor's still kind of slippery and slidey."

"Come on in," Catherine called to Jason and Maura.

"We'll finish our discussion later," Monica insisted under her breath to Catherine before going to take the salad bowl from Maura.

"No, we won't," Catherine returned just as quietly, tossing her hair out of her face with an exasperated motion. Honestly, sometimes Monica could be downright scary. Catherine crossed over to Jason and relieved him of the paper plates, cups and two liters of pop he'd brought as an additional offering. "Thank you," she said, smiling up at him. "This was very thoughtful."

"You're welcome," Jason replied. "I'm afraid it was all I could come up with in terms of an impromptu housewarming gift."

"It's perfect," Catherine assured him, already unscrewing the cap on the cola bottle. "It's been a distressing day. I could use a jolt of caffeine right about now." She gave Monica a meaningful look.

"I bet. Here, let me do that," Jason said, pulling several cups out of the plastic sleeve they'd come wrapped in. "How about your husband and your friend? What would they like?"

"What husband?" Catherine asked, as she watched his strong hands take over the task of pouring drinks. "Oh, you mean *him?* Donald? That's not my husband—"

"Kindly refrain from referring to me as a *that,*" Don interjected. He'd already confiscated the paper plates and was spooning out large quantities of rice onto one. "I am a *he,* at least I was before I started withering up and dying from lack of nutrition."

"That grouch over there," Catherine indicated, as though her brother-in-law hadn't spoken, "belongs to my sister, Monica. She actually loves him.'' Catherine pointed in Monica's direction. ''Amy is theirs.''

Jason took a quick look around the kitchen, then leaned slightly back to glance down the hallway that bisected the front of the house. He hadn't missed anybody. ''Then you're not—?''

Catherine shook her head in a determinedly cheerful manner. ''Nope, I'm not married. Free as a breeze.'' There was a brief flash of panic crossing her new neighbor's face, and Catherine knew he was envisioning being hunted. She almost laughed out loud. The man would die if he knew how close he was to being right, provided Monica got her way.

A quick look behind Jason brought Monica into focus. Her sister's eyes were crossed in an obvious sign of disapproval. Monica must have thought she was being too flippant. Too bad. Catherine would be nice to the man, friendly, but only because he had a daughter she was pretty sure she'd enjoy being around. The child seemed to be such a stereotypical preadolescent it was downright funny, at least from Catherine's point of view. But she was not going to bother struggling to understand the male mind again. No way. Forget it.

''You're blowing it,'' Monica whispered as she passed by on her way to the table. ''Subtlety is the key here. We're only planting seeds, remember?''

''Put a sock in it, Mon,'' Catherine advised her sister cheerfully. ''I don't care if I blow it or not. I'm implementing plan B whether you approve or not.''

Monica, however, was not to be deterred. She switched to a high-beam smile as Jason approached the table, several cups of soda held firmly between his two large hands.

"Here we go, everybody," Jason said heartily. "Pop all around." But underneath the external good cheer, he just wanted to eat and get out of there. He'd been hunted too many times both before and after his divorce not to be nervous about having a single woman move in next door. He was not interested. No sirree, not him. There was no such thing as happily ever after. He'd learned that the hard way. He might take the chance if he was on his own and he'd be the only one paying the price for failure, but Maura had had enough upheaval in her young life. He was off the playing field until Maura was safely grown.

He looked at Catherine Nicholson as she sipped her drink and almost groaned out loud. It would be tough going if they had to spend any time together. No mistaking it, this was one extremely attractive woman. Even all hot and bothered looking from her rough day, Catherine exuded sex appeal. Now that his heart had dropped back down into his chest after his daughter's disappearing act, he could see that. A good woman to steer clear of, as a matter of fact. At least until his head could convince the lower part of his body to swallow the company line he was trying to feed it.

He despaired over the injustices of life. Why couldn't she be safely married? Or if she had to be single, why couldn't she be ugly? But no, there was absolutely nothing harsh or unattractive about her. Hair the color of ripe chestnuts curled under gently along her jawline and it angled up toward the back of her head, forming a saucy high wedge. Her eyes were a soft, medium brown framed by thick spiky lashes, and her skin was creamy and without blemish. There was not even a single freckle with enough nerve to marr the smooth arch of her high cheekbones. And her body was nicely padded in all the places a man appreciated a bit of padding. He didn't know if he could handle having that body right next door, unattached, available for pursuing. He ground his teeth in frustration.

You, Jason silently informed himself, had just better be on your guard. You cannot even begin to entertain the type of prurient thoughts you are already considering. Not while Maura is at such an impressionable age. Just stop it.

Jason consciously averted his eyes from Catherine's cameo profile and sat. Catherine handed him the Mongolian beef container, so he was forced to turn his head briefly in her direction, but as soon as he had a firm grip on the carton, he returned his eyes to look directly in front of him. "Thanks."

"You're welcome."

After checking around that everyone else had a plateful, Jason spooned a large amount of rice onto his plate, then topped it with an equally large amount of the beef. He tore the top off a little plastic envelope of soy and squeezed that liberally over the mound and picked up his fork. Jason had it loaded and halfway to his mouth when something Maura said earlier clicked and he dropped the fork with a clatter.

"The crib," he said before he could think how it would sound. "You have a baby?"

Jason cringed. He didn't mean to sound judgmental, but he was already attracted to her. And he could tell Maura had taken an interest in her, as well. He was not unaware of the lack of feminine guidance in his daughter's life, he just didn't know what to do about it. He had no sisters, and his former wife had "gotten on with her life," an event that seemed to exclude her own daughter. It just might be good for Maura to spend some time with Amy and her aunt. They seemed close. But not if the woman had no morals.

"Are you divorced?" he asked hopefully. That would explain a baby.

"Divorced?" Catherine asked. "No, I'm not divorced. I've never been married. And I don't have a baby. Where'd you get that idea?"

"But you moved in a crib," Maura said, obviously confused. "I saw it. I was going to ask you if I could baby-sit for you. I took the Red Cross baby-sitting course and everything."

"The crib," Monica repeated, sounding a bit panicky to Catherine's ears. "That's easy to explain."

Catherine's eyes widened at that. It was? This she had to hear.

"It's an heirloom," Monica announced baldly, and Catherine blinked at the blatant lie. "Handed down through my, um, mother's side for several generations.

Don looked up from his rapidly shrinking mountain of cashew chicken. "It is?" he asked in surprise. "I thought it was another one from the shop."

"Well you thought wrong," his wife told him.

"How come we didn't use it?" her spouse continued.

"Because it's an heirloom handed down to the

youngest daughter of the family, that's why," Monica informed him in a rather severe voice.

"Oh," Don said, nodding wisely. "Your family always was a little weird. Sounds like something strange they'd come up with." His interest returned to his plate of food, and Catherine breathed a sigh of relief. This was the reason she rarely lied. Somehow the lie always snowballed, and you ended up a nervous wreck while you tried to keep things plausible and remain undiscovered in your deceit. In the process, your digestive juices turned on your stomach wall and before you knew it, *presto*, instant ulcer. Before she could check Jason's face to see if he'd swallowed Monica's ridiculous explanation, Amy interrupted.

"Aunt Cath?"

"Yes, Amy?"

"You know how we were going shopping and out to lunch on Saturday so you could get your kid fix?"

Jason's head snapped up. He stared first at Amy, then at Catherine.

Across the table Catherine could see Monica's eyes were closed and she was shaking her head. "Uh, yeah. What about it?" Not only did she now owe Monica another favor—since Amy had just made it clear they had already made plans together for Saturday, and it wasn't to pay Monica back for helping today—but even a quick sideways glance in Jason's direction told her he was back on red alert. Well, too bad. That was his problem. He'd figure out she wasn't interested sooner or later. Meanwhile it was sort of entertaining, in a perverse sort of way, to watch him squirm.

"Well, maybe Maura could come with us. That way," she continued brightly, "I'd have a friend and you could get a *double* kid fix all for one trip to the mall. Wouldn't that be cool?"

Catherine propped her elbow on the table, her chin in her hand, while she considered the idea. Actually, it wasn't bad. "Two for the price of one, huh? Sure, why not? It's okay with me if it's okay with Maura's dad."

"Kid fix?" Jason questioned, raising a rather formidable brow at her.

Catherine gave him an arch look in return. Let him think what he liked. "I enjoy kids. So what? Just because I'm unmarried and have no children of my own does not mean I don't appreciate their company and value their friendship."

"Yeah, Dad, some people *like* being around kids."

"Some people aren't responsible for a child's formation and upbringing. They can afford to let down their guard and just have fun. I'd love to kick back and relax with you, Maura. Unfortunately, I've got all the responsibilities of being both parents to you, and that's got to take precedence."

Catherine smiled at Maura. "He's got you there, sweet cheeks. When I've had my kid fix for the day, or you get bratty, I can just send you home and go on my merry way. Your dad can't do that. He's in it for the long haul and deserves a lot of respect. Having fun with you is the easy part. Disciplining is hard, though. And judging by what I can see, your dad's doing one heck of a job."

Maura looked doubtful, but Amy cut in. "So she can come?"

"If you don't mind sharing, it's okay with me, but like I said, Maura will have to get her father's permission."

Maura clasped her hands in front of her. "Please, Daddy," she pleaded. "You can't object to this. She's a grown-up and everything."

Giving permission would get him out of the doghouse with his darling progeny, but darn it, Saturday was his day to spend quality time with Maura. Not that his daughter wouldn't probably have a better time without him around—which hurt. "Maura, I'd be willing to take you to the mall. I've offered several times—"

"But I want to go with Amy and her Aunt Cath. Please?" his daughter begged.

"I thought you and I could do something together that day. If you don't want to go to the mall with me, maybe we could—"

Monica cleared her throat and smiled. "I've got an idea," she said, sounding very much like the cat that swallowed the cream. "Why don't you go along with them, Jason? The four of you could all go together and spend the day at the mall. Go to lunch. Maybe even see a movie if you get shopped out." Monica shot an ingenuous smile at her sister.

Catherine blinked. She'd been outmaneuvered. Darn her sister's rotten hide. "Jason might not be comfortable spending his day with three women, Monica. You know how men are about shopping. You shouldn't put him on the spot like that."

Jason sighed. This really was not the way he wanted to spend half of his precious weekend. Still, it was probably the only way he'd spend time with

Maura without getting himself further into the doghouse. "No, it's all right," he said. "I'd be a fool to turn down the opportunity to escort three such beautiful women anywhere, even the mall. I'll drive. I'll even spring for lunch."

"Dad!" Maura wailed. "Everything will be wrecked if you come along!"

Jason rolled his eyes. "Maura, I happen to know that the only time you even acknowledge my presence when we're out in public is when it's time to get out the credit cards. Otherwise I'm pretty much just a background fixture. How will my coming along ruin things?" He already knew the answer. It just didn't make any sense to him.

"Because you're my father!" his daughter cried. "Couldn't you just give me some money and let me go with them?"

Jason rubbed his eyes tiredly. He wanted to be a friend to his daughter, God knew he did. Was it his fault Maura kept pushing him into the roll of disciplinarian? "Maura," he began patiently, "by choosing to force the issue here and now instead of waiting until we're alone and could talk this out, you've put me in the position where I'll have to speak plainly and possibly embarrass you and your friend."

Maura's eyes widened in consternation.

"You've been wanting to go to the mall, and I have offered several times to take you. Here's an opportunity for you to get what you want. But Saturday is my day to spend some time with you. I'm afraid you're going to have to suffer my company or lose the trip."

Maura's lower lip was stuck out about a half a yard,

Jason thought as he measured it with his eyes. This was one unhappy little girl. "Come on, honey, give a little, get a little. You're going to have to learn the fine art of compromise."

Catherine decided to put in her two cents' worth. She was unwillingly starting to like and respect this Jason Engel. He wasn't afraid to stick to his guns, not even in the face of some formidable preadolescent resistance. "Your dad's right, Maura. You're a very lucky girl that he cares enough to be so careful of you. Let's give him a break and let him come along. Next time we'll make it all girls, all right?"

Maura looked to Amy for final approval.

Amy shrugged.

Maura turned to Catherine and her father and reluctantly nodded. "Okay, I guess."

Jason felt like he'd just won a major victory. He wanted to stand up and shout alleluia, possibly turn a few cartwheels, but he merely nodded at his daughter to indicate he'd heard. "Ten o'clock Saturday morning?" he asked Catherine.

"Sounds good," Catherine said.

Jason looked at his plate. Somehow, in the midst of all the negotiations, he'd managed to clean it up. He pushed back his chair. "Good. Maura and I will pick you and Amy up. But for now we'll help you clean up, and then I'm afraid we've got to get going. Maura's got homework to do and I've got some paperwork waiting for me. Maura, you clear the table and put all the plates in the trash, and I'll close up the containers and stash them in the fridge."

"You don't have to—"

"We insist, don't we, Maura?" Her dad arched that impressive brow in his daughter's direction.

"But—"

"Forget it, Ms. Nicholson," Maura said, whisking Catherine's plate away from in front of her. "Dad's a real stickler about not taking advantage and always pitching in when somebody's done something nice for you."

"Oh, well..."

The table was cleared and the leftover takeout already in the refrigerator. Catherine was still in her chair. The man worked fast. She'd have to remember that. "I guess I'll see you Saturday, then," she said weakly.

Jason nodded, Maura was more verbose. She had her arm around Amy, and they walked to the door together. "We'll still have fun on Saturday, even with my dad along," Maura bubbled, her head close to Amy's. "You'll see. There's just this one little problem I need to figure out." She looked furtively over her shoulder.

Jason was no more than two steps behind. It would have been impossible not to hear, but he was getting good at pretending. In dealing with a preadolescent, he had discovered it was the better part of valor. There were enough big things you had to make a stand on that if you included the non-life-threatening stuff, as well, there'd never be a moment's peace. So, he kept his head up and his eyes straight ahead, pretending not to hear. If his daughter thought she and her friend were going to ditch him once they hit the mall, they had another think coming.

"We'll talk about it at school," Maura told her

friend, much to Jason's disappointment. Oh, well, Maura wasn't very good at keeping secrets. He'd find out sooner or later.

Catherine's store was closed Mondays, which was why she'd chosen it as a moving day. The next morning found her back at her shop, Hand Arounds, doing her best to concentrate on the work in front of her rather than on the boxes waiting to be unpacked at her new house.

"Yes, I'm quite sure that you paid $16.00 for that blouse brand-new, Mrs. Conroy, but I'll only be able to get $3.00 for it secondhand, which means I can only pay you $1.50 for it. The jumper would be $3.50 and I'd be able to do $1.50 for the pants. See where they're slightly frayed? If you want to change your mind about selling your daughter's things, I understand, but I'm afraid that's the best I can do."

While Catherine waited for the balking Mrs. Conroy to make up her mind, she thought about Jason Engel.

Was her sister right?

No, of course not. Monica was a nutcase. She was never right.

Well, she wasn't totally wrong, either, Catherine admitted. The idea of trying to find a sperm bank and implement her idea was nerve-racking as all get-out. That much she'd give Monica. But Jason Engel as husband and father of her dream child? Uh-uh. No way. She'd liked Gerald, but the decision to marry him had been almost intellectual. She'd weighed the pros and cons carefully then made her choice. Her heart had been involved, certainly, but not to the extent that her feelings had overridden her intellect.

Somehow she doubted she'd get away with such lukewarm responses to any involvement with Jason Engel. Which meant that if she ever lost her heart to a virile specimen like that, she'd certainly never recover.

Catherine rang up two pair of booties at seventy-five cents each and a terry cloth sleeper for $2.50 while she pondered the problem.

She liked Maura. Under all that preadolescent angst, Maura was a decent kid who'd turn out just fine provided her dad stayed on top of things. She had a pretty little face. She'd seen it when the child had briefly stopped scowling. It would be nice if Catherine's baby, when she came, had hair as nice and thick as Maura's.

The girl had nice-colored eyes, too. They matched her dad's, and the gene for brown was dominant. She could live with that, Catherine decided. Especially if they came with the same dark, spiky lashes that Maura had.

Catherine made change for a five-dollar bill and handed over the sack of clothing. "Thanks. You come in again. We get new merchandise all the time. Still thinking, Mrs. Conroy? No problem. I'm not going anywhere. Take your time."

When it came right down to it, Catherine would like a daughter just like Maura Engel. Maybe what she should do is simply make a list cataloging all the things she liked about Jason and Maura and present it at the sperm bank. See if they had anything that would come close. She sure would like a little girl baby that would grow up with all the promise of beauty that Maura Engel displayed. Catherine looked over at the rack of pink sleepers in the newborn section.

Yes, she sure would like that.

Chapter Three

Catherine thought of little else but her new neighbor
for the next two days. It didn't really affect her work.
She could sort baby things in her sleep. Someone
brought in a pair of little booties crocheted to look
like brown-and-white saddle shoes complete with
baby blue socks, and a second pair that looked like
Mary Janes also having the sock crocheted right into
the pattern. They were too cute to sell. Catherine paid
the woman two bucks a pair and brought them home
with her Thursday after she closed the shop. She put
them up in the spare bedroom with the still-unas-
sembled "heirloom" crib. Then she called her sister.

"Monica? Hi, it's Cath. I've been thinking. Since
my next-door neighbor seems to have taken over this
trip to the mall and claimed driving privileges before
I could open my mouth, maybe it would be best if
Amy stayed overnight tomorrow night. What do you
think?"

"Sounds like fun. Don's got some kind of business function that'll probably last till late. Maybe I'll come, too, but just for the evening. We could order in pizza and rent a chick flick, just the three of us. You don't think Amy's too young for a girls' night out, do you?"

"Depends on the flick we pick."

There was a thoughtful pause. "Yeah. Well, we'll be careful, that's all." Monica cleared her throat delicately. "Uh, Cath, I've been doing a little investigating for you."

Catherine closed her eyes and leaned against the kitchen wall for support. "No. Tell me you haven't been out there asking obvious questions and embarrassing me. Monica, how could you?"

"Take it easy, I didn't use your name. I said it was for a friend."

"Oh, yeah, right. We've only lived here forever. Anybody you asked knows me and is going to put two and two together real quick."

"Will you stop? What's done is done. Now just listen to what I've found out. Cath?"

"What?" Catherine concentrated on opening a can of soup. She poured it into a bowl and stuck the bowl in the microwave. She remembered to take the spoon out at the last second.

"I really wish you'd at least consider waiting a bit longer, see if there's a chance of things working out with the new next-door neighbor or somebody else before, you know, you go do the other thing."

Catherine took her soup out of the microwave and stirred it a bit. "You mean before I go to the sperm bank?"

"Yes. The information I got isn't complete, you know, because I was being so subtle and everything, but what it boils down to is there are a few things we failed to consider the other night when we were talking about this."

Catherine retrieved the bowl of soup and carefully sipped a spoonful. "Like what?"

"Your ob-gyn is the one who would know where the closest sperm bank is. In fact, you'd probably have to get a referral from him, I bet. At least that's what Alice Moran thought."

"Oh, God, you weren't talking to Alice about this, were you? Tell me you didn't do that to me."

"Yes, I did, and I can't unask her, so cool it and think about what she said. It makes sense."

Catherine forgot to blow on the next spoonful in her agitation and ended up burning her mouth. "Oh, damn," she moaned. "Monica, I've been going to him for years. He *knows* I'm not married. What's he going to think?"

"That you want a baby. Come on, Catherine, even if you go the live male route, you're still going to have to get prenatal care. He's going to figure it out either way. I'm telling you, if you stick to doing things the way you're talking about, there's a lot of this kind of thing you're going to be faced with."

Catherine slumped over the countertop. "Oh, God. This is all getting to be too much. I had planned to find a place where nobody knew me and I didn't know anybody and have it done, I don't know—anonymously."

"I get the feeling that if you want to be anonymous

about this, you're going to have to wear a bag over your head,'' Monica warned.

Catherine poured the rest of the soup down the disposal, unable to finish it now. Well, she'd known the sperm bank approach would be clinical and unromantic. But then again, there wasn't much romantic about finding out your fiancé was two-timing you, either. So she'd cope with the embarrassment. There was no viable alternative as far as she was concerned. "I'll think about it," she said, knowing she wouldn't.

"That's all I ask. We'll come by around six-thirty tomorrow night, okay? That should give you just enough time to get home. I'll order the pizza on my way out the door so you'll have time to change before it gets there.''

"Fine. Thanks.''

"See you then.''

Catherine hung up the phone feeling disgruntled and put upon. Man, this simple little project—having a baby—was starting to develop a life of its own and turn ugly on her. How was she ever going to work up the courage to do this?

"I'll pick up some paint Saturday afternoon after we're back from the mall," she told herself as she rinsed out her soup bowl. "Yellow. That can go either way, boy or girl. I'll paint the nursery and set up the crib. That'll make it more real and give me courage.''

With that, she turned out the lights and went upstairs to run her hand along the beautiful canopy crib leaning against one of the walls. Then she took out the Mary Jane booties and studied them for several minutes. Baby things. Her baby's things. Her up-until-she-did-something-about-it, nonexistent baby's things.

She went to bed, exhausted.

Amy and Monica showed up promptly at six-thirty the next night, the pizza man on their heels.

"Well, you two certainly didn't waste any time getting here."

"Heck no, we're starved," Amy informed her aunt. "We got a bag of baby carrots at the store and some crackers with spinach dip. Mom says we have to have more vegetables than just the tomato sauce on the pizza."

"Sounds reasonable, I guess."

"Did Maura call yet?"

Catherine's brows rose. "No, are we expecting her to?"

Amy shrugged out of her windbreaker and dropped it on the floor by the kitchen door next to her sleeping bag and a plastic bag with her pillow and overnight stuff. "Well, yeah. I happened to mention that Mom and I were coming over here, and she was going to see if her dad would let her come over for the pizza and movie part and then maybe even sleep over, if it's okay with you. You always fall asleep so early, Aunt Cath, you know you do."

Catherine glanced at her sister. "Did she just tell me that I'm getting old?"

Monica shrugged and set the pizza she'd taken from the delivery boy on the kitchen countertop. "You already knew it, anyway, Cath. Isn't that why you decided on an alternate route to your goal?"

"I know, but—"

"Pick up your coat, Amy. You dropped it on the floor right underneath the hook where it's supposed to be hung. How much extra time would it have taken to put it where it belonged instead of on the floor where someone will step on it...and right after I just washed it?"

"Don't worry, Mom, nobody's going to walk on it."

"I'll make a point of walking on it myself if you don't hang it up."

Amy seemed unconcerned. She lifted the corner of the pizza box and sniffed deeply. "You'd just be creating more work for yourself, because then you'd only have to wash it again. Can we eat now?"

Catherine had to turn her head to keep from laughing at her sister's frustration. Monica's eyes had narrowed to slits. "Pick the coat up *now,* Amy Marie."

Amy rolled her eyes and stomped back over to the door. She snatched her jacket off the floor and jammed it onto a hook. "There. Satisfied?"

Monica, paragon of virtue that she was, simply nodded and said, "Yes. Thank you. Now you can have some pizza." Then, with her daughter safely occupied stuffing her face, she turned to glare at Catherine. "You can afford to laugh now," she whispered to her sister, "but just wait. If you go through with this you'll find out. Babies are just like kittens and puppies. They grow up and turn into—" Monica waved a disdainful hand at her own progeny "—that."

"You mean a typical teenager?"

Monica shuddered. "Yes. And let me tell you, it's a whole lot easier to put up with when they're just visiting, and you can send them back to wherever they came from when you feel the need for some peace and quiet. It's a different story when there's no place to go to escape them. Twenty-four hours a day, they're *there* right on top of you, driving you nuts, making you question your own sanity."

"All right, okay. I get the picture. She's getting on your nerves today. Once Maura gets here and the movie is on we won't hear a peep out of them for a couple of hours. Very restorative." Catherine patted her sister's arm. "Now get yourself a slice of pizza. It'll make you feel better."

There was a knock on the back door. Without looking, Catherine yelled, "Amy, Maura's here."

Amy flew into the kitchen, opened the door and dragged Maura Engel inside. "Great. I'm so glad you're here. Fix a plate and let's go start the movie."

"Hi, Ms. Nicholson."

Catherine smiled and turned around, prepared to greet her young neighbor. "Hi, Mau—oh, Jason, you're here too. How...nice. Come in. Can I interest you in some pizza?" Catherine asked politely.

Jason stood by the back door, looking incredibly good in jeans and a heavy wool sweater. "No, thank you. I'll get something at home."

"There's more than enough."

"Thanks, but I'm not going to horn in on an all-girls' night. I just wanted to double-check that this was really okay with you and that you weren't being railroaded into anything."

Catherine nodded approvingly. "I understand. And you also wanted to make sure I was actually going to be here, that there'd be an adult on the scene."

"Well, yeah."

"Yes, I'll be here all night. Monica's leaving after the movie, but I have no plans to go out."

"Good. I mean, fine, then. I'll...see you tomorrow, I guess. Here's Maura's sleeping bag and a pillow. Send her home early if you want. She can eat breakfast at home. I, well, I'll see you."

"Bye." Catherine waved. She shrugged fatalistically at the closed back door. Jason Engel couldn't wait to get out of there. He'd done his parental duty and taken off. She absolutely wasn't hurt by that. No, indeed. This way Monica would see how hopeless her idea was. Jason Engel was not Prince Charming. She lifted the lid of the pizza box and removed a piece. Catherine severed her cheese strands from the main body of pizza and walked out of the room. Just think. In a few months she probably wouldn't be able to eat a pizza supreme. Pepperoni, sausage, green pepper—probably make her sick as a dog. She could hardly wait.

Monica grabbed some pizza and baby carrots and followed Catherine into the family room, scowling all the while, but Catherine knew she was safe enough from any more lectures. Monica wouldn't say anything in front of the girls. And she was right.

"What're we watching?" Monica asked after she'd flounced onto the sofa.

"This movie my friend Annette told me about," Amy responded, already engrossed in the opening scene. "She said it was totally the best ever."

Catherine bit off a good-size chunk of pizza and concentrated on chewing it. Ten minutes into the movie, Catherine knew it was hopeless. It required concentration to follow a plot this dumb, and she didn't have any. Jason Engel kept jumping into her mind, his formfitting blue jeans molding his rear and the soft brown wool sweater showing off both his eyes and his ridiculously broad shoulders.

Twenty minutes later, Catherine gave up. She left the room and came back with her quilting hoop. She sat on the sofa, legs tucked up beneath her and determinedly jammed her needle into the fabric.

Maura glanced up from her sprawl on the floor. "What're you making, Ms. Nicholson?" she asked, rising and coming over for a better look.

"It's a wall hanging," Catherine admitted. And because it was ridiculous to try to disguise it, the theme being teddy bears having a picnic, she added, "For a nursery."

"Oh, it's so cute. Are you going to sell it in your shop? I thought Amy said you only sold secondhand children's things."

Monica was looking panicked, and Catherine thought to lie just so she wouldn't get yelled at later. "Ordinarily that's true, but—"

"Aunt Cath has always wanted to have a kid," Amy interrupted matter-of-factly, her foot swinging as she stared at the television. "It's why she keeps borrowing me. Now that you live next door, she'll probably borrow you a lot, too."

Catherine checked Maura out of the corner of her eye. She looked pleased. Good. "Amy, I think—"

"The thing is," Amy continued blithely, "you and I are getting old. We're really not children any longer."

No, they were full-fledged preadolescent pains. At least Amy was. "Amy—"

"So I heard Mom telling Dad that Aunt Cath is going to go ahead and decorate her own nursery and try and get a baby. Isn't that cool?"

Maura agreed. "Oh, wow. Amy and I'll baby-sit for you. This is so awesome. How long do you think it will take before you get your baby? I heard sometimes adoptions can take a long time 'cuz there's a shortage of good babies out there."

"Uh—"

"No, no, she's not going to adopt. She wants one all of her own. We've got to find her a man before she goes and does something stupid. That's what my mom said."

"Amy Marie, that's quite enough," Monica finally said severely, and far too late in Catherine's opinion. "Haven't you ever heard the word *discretion?*"

"No, what's it mean?"

Catherine ignored her niece. She'd like to ignore her sister, as well—for the rest of her life. No wonder Amy didn't know the meaning of *discretion.* She concentrated on Maura instead. "It means this is going to be our little secret. All right, Maura? It's kind of a private thing for me. I'm not sure other people would understand."

Maura was enthralled by the idea of not only babies, but keeping secrets. "Oh, I understand," she said breathlessly. "I want triplets when I get married. Maybe even quadruplets. But everybody always laughs when I say that, so I don't tell anybody anymore."

"That's 'cuz it's dumb," Amy contributed as she

avidly watched the bully get his comeuppance. "It's too hard to take care of that many babies all by yourself. I only want twins. Two sets."

Catherine was desperate to stop the conversation. "Here, Maura, sit down and I'll let you sew on this for a while. I'll work on the crib bumpers instead. Just remember, you can't breathe a word of this to anyone, not if you want me to let you help decorate the nursery."

"I promise," the child pledged as she sat next to Catherine. "Not a word. This is so cool. Now I'll know how to do it for my babies."

Monica left at eleven, and Catherine shepherded the girls to bed by midnight. She woke them at eight the next morning.

Amy opened one eye and looked at her. "Are you sure it's morning?"

"Positive. Come on, morning glory, rise and shine."

Amy reluctantly rolled out of her sleeping bag and stretched. "Listen, Aunt Cath," she said as she and Maura sleepily followed Catherine down the stairs to the first floor.

"Both of you hold the rail as you go down," Catherine instructed. "Your eyes are still half-shut. I'm afraid you're going to stumble and fall down the stairs."

And in fact, the two of them were so out of it, they forgot to argue and simply did as they were told. "Listen, Aunt Cath, before Mr. Engel gets here I've got to tell you something really important. It's about today and Maura and her dad and everything. I was going to ask you last night, but you fell asleep before the second movie was over.''

Uh-oh. Now what? "Let's get some cereal into you. You can tell me whatever it is while you eat." Please don't let it be too awful, Catherine silently prayed. She wanted to spend time with the girls, but not if they were going to try and put her in the middle of anything, use her to play Maura off against her dad.

She ushered them into the kitchen and pulled several boxes of cereal down from a cabinet. "Here. Pick something while I get us some bowls and the milk."

Catherine was not surprised when Amy reached for the most heavily sugared variety. "Get a banana from the bowl in the corner and slice up at least half of one into of your bowl. I just know your mother's going to want to know what I fed you. Fruit makes it sound a little better balanced, I think."

"Okay, but, Aunt Cath, about this problem with Maura—''

Catherine plopped the carton of milk down on the table. "What about it? Why don't you let Maura speak for herself?"

"I—I think I'll run home and have breakfast with my dad," Maura said suddenly. "He doesn't like to eat alone. He told me he enjoys my company at mealtimes and that's why I have to always be home by six, no matter what. Families eat together, he says. Besides, Amy promised she'd ask you for me. It's too embarrassing and she did promise."

"All right, okay. Go eat with your dad so he doesn't get lonely. We'll be ready in a little while."

"Thanks," Maura gushed, her relief evident. "I

had a great time. Explain how important this is, Amy. I'll just die, otherwise. And I'll be your best friend forever. Bye.''

The door slammed shut behind Maura, and Catherine turned and arched a brow at Amy. "Well?"

"Well, here's the thing. The *real* reason she doesn't want her dad to come along—besides the fact that it's only totally mortifying for your father to be taking you shopping at our age—is that Maura needs some teen bras. I mean, Mom took me shopping for mine the end of sixth grade and that was bad enough, but can you imagine going out for something like that with your *dad?* And besides, Maura can't talk to her dad about it. She just can't. She's only been living with him for a little over a year. Before that she lived with her mom, but then her mom got remarried and her stepdad didn't want her around 'cuz he had kids of his own and said he didn't think it would work out to keep both sets of kids, so she came here.''

Amy took a deep breath, for which Catherine was grateful. She was having a little trouble following the convoluted story and it gave her a moment to catch up.

"So, like, she's not real comfortable talking with her dad about stuff like bras and things, and now she's the only one in the locker room when we change for gym that's still wearing an undershirt. She doesn't think her dad has even noticed that she's—you know.'' Amy made a gesture over her chest Catherine assumed was meant to indicate breasts.

She stared at her niece, her cereal forgotten and rapidly growing soggy in front of her. "Let me get this straight. Am I to assume that you and Maura want me to discuss Maura's underwear crisis with her father, a man I don't know from Adam?'' Catherine rubbed her temples. Her life was becoming extremely complicated. She barely knew this man, but her sister wanted her to marry him, and his daughter wanted her to discuss intimate apparel with him. Good God. She needed an aspirin. She suspected Jason would, too, if he ever came to suspect even half of this. As a matter of fact, maybe she'd bring the bottle along. This might prove to be a trying kind of day.

''I—''

Amy's words were interrupted by the ringing of the doorbell.

''Run upstairs, comb your hair and wash your face,'' Catherine directed as she swept the cereal bowls away. ''I'll have to think about this a little bit.''

She went to answer the door. Maura hadn't been living with Jason for all that long? Her own mother had let some self-centered jerk tell her to ship her daughter off so that she could concentrate on his children instead? And she'd let him? What was wrong with that woman that she'd give up a sweetheart like Maura? Catherine was shaking her head as she opened the door.

And there he was. It was like looking at the sun. She almost had to squint, he was so gorgeous. She studied him wistfully wondering if by any remote possibility he might have a few frozen you-know-what on deposit at the local sperm bank that she could get her hands on. She blushed at the very thought. Have Jason's baby? The very idea made her shiver—and not with revulsion.

''Hi,'' she managed to say, ready to kill her sister

for having planted the seeds of her prurient thoughts in her head. "We're almost ready."

Jason stood outside Catherine's back door. He'd met the woman just last night, but there must have been something wrong with the lighting, or something. Damn, but she was cute. Not pretty or beautiful in the classical sense, she was too short for that, but cute as all get-out. He cocked his head as he studied her. Why was she looking at him so oddly? Did he have something on his face?

"Is there something wrong?" he asked Catherine. "Did I miss a spot of shaving cream?"

Oh, God, he shaved with a real razor. It seemed so *macho*, somehow. "Uh, no, there's nothing wrong. We're almost ready." Catherine turned away from the door and called, "Amy. Oh, there you are. Grab your jacket, honey. We're holding up the show here."

Catherine got her purse and jacket. By the time she'd carefully locked her door and was ready to leave, Maura and Amy were already headed toward Jason's garage, giggling, talking and casting nervous glances over their shoulders. Catherine was left to walk with Jason.

"Looks like they're already making plans to run us ragged," Jason remarked as he guided Catherine across the grass with a hand under her arm.

Catherine had never felt so petite as she did with Jason Engel standing next to her, dwarfing her. She could feel the heat of his hand right through the sleeve of her jacket and the sweater she wore beneath it. It was no surprise to discover he was hot-blooded.

"My feet hurt already," Catherine agreed, smiling at the backs of the two chattering girls.

Jason politely handed her into the passenger front seat and closed the door. He walked around and slid behind the steering wheel. "We're off," he said, checking that the two girls had their seat belts on as he started backing down his driveway.

The conversation was only slightly strained as Jason drove in the direction of the mall. If Catherine could only think of a way to subtly bring up Maura's bra situation, maybe the day wouldn't be so bad after all. It was lost in terms of a kid fix—Amy and Maura had all but forgotten her presence, but she'd like to at least get comfortable with Jason so her whole day wasn't spent on edge.

Catherine was about to attempt—casually—changing the conversation from the cool fall weather to preadolescent changing bodies when Jason drove by a church parking lot. "Oh, my gosh, can we stop here? Please?"

Jason shot her a startled glance. "Stop here? What for? You don't get carsick, do you?" He couldn't pull over fast enough.

A groan reverberated from the back seat. "No, it's much worse than that," Amy said. "Look at the sign. That church is having a rummage sale. Once she gets sucked in there, it'll be hours before we get her back under control. Don't do it, Mr. Engel."

"Why, Amy Marie Davies," Catherine said, "that is patently untrue. One time when you were with me, *one time* I spent slightly over an hour because they had lots of good children's and baby stuff to go through, and you've never let me forget it. All I want is half an hour today. Just half an hour, then I swear we'll leave, no matter what. You and Maura can go through the books or the tapes if you don't want to help me—even though I'm going out of my way for the two of you today, in case you've both forgotten—but don't worry about that. I'm perfectly willing to do all the work by myself. Just give me half an hour.''

Jason had already turned into the church's parking lot. He knew a lost cause when it hit him in the face. But he had a sick feeling in the pit of his stomach. *He* was the one that was going to get ill. Jason pulled into a spot and switched the key off, then looked over at Catherine. "You want to go in there and buy baby clothes? What for?" She'd said she wasn't married. She'd said she had no children. But he and Maura had seen a crib being moved in. Was it an heirloom or wasn't it? Was the block going to have a blessed addition in a few months?

"I own a secondhand children's store, Jason. There are a lot of good finds at sales like these. Sometimes I don't need to do anything but wash an item, others require some soaking in a strong stain remover first, but I can usually find enough good stuff to wash up and resell that is well worth my while."

Oh. Well. So maybe he'd overreacted a little bit. He certainly had enough reason, the way he'd been chased since his divorce. He sighed. "Let's get it over with, then. You can pick out the things you want. I'll have a cup of coffee or something."

"It'd go a lot faster if you help, too, Dad," his daughter said. "It'll be fun looking through the baby stuff, don't you think, Amy?"

Amy got Maura sidetracked again, for which Jason was grateful. Looking at baby things would probably have him breaking out in hives. He was allergic to baby things, he was sure. There was no way he could help sort through them without turning green around the gills, he just knew it.

So he set the timer on his wristwatch for thirty minutes, exactly, although he held little hope of actually leaving at the end of the allotted time—women were so pathetic when it came to baby stuff. He knew from experience they could wallow in it for hours and went to find some coffee so he could tank up on enough caffeine to get him through the rest of the day.

Chapter Four

"Oh, isn't this adorable?" Amy cooed as she held up a ruffled baby bonnet.

"Look at this, Aunt Cath. I found four baby blankets and a pink newborn-size sacque. I wish I wasn't too old to play with dolls now. I bet this would fit Baby Betsy just right."

Catherine happened to know that Amy still took out Baby Betsy when she thought nobody would notice. "Why don't you take the sacque, anyway, Amy? And the pink-and-white blanket. Put them away with Baby Betsy. Maybe your own children will enjoy them someday."

Or you, yourself, next time you sneak Baby Betsy out, Catherine thought. She looked over to Maura who wore a similar dreamy look that had Catherine smiling.

"Oh, that's a good idea," Maura said. "Do it, Amy. I think I'm going to keep some of the stuff I found and put it away with my old baby doll, too. Maybe I'll let my children use her, if they promise to be careful. Baby Maureen is a Madame Alexander, so my mom made sure I took real good care of her. I hardly ever got to play with her myself.''

That from Maura, his very own flesh and blood, Jason thought as he came up behind them. Jason had just sought the women out after finishing his second cup of coffee.

Oh, God. Jason thought he was going to choke. Catherine's little side trip was going to kill him. He thought baby things were okay. Once upon a time he'd been a sucker for those little items, he remembered. Maura had certainly looked adorable in the things he and Karen had purchased for her. But looking at them didn't make him want to run out and have one. Just listen to these three planning and putting things away for their mythical progeny. Granted it was kind of cute, but it was also scary the effect a teeny-tiny undershirt or a baby rattle had on a woman.

Maybe Karen had attended one too many baby showers. Maybe that was why she'd insisted on getting pregnant when Jason hadn't felt they were quite stable enough as a couple to take on nurturing another life just yet. Several of Karen's friends had either produced babies or at the very least announced pregnancies just before Karen had gotten pregnant. Karen had spent a lot of time in the baby sections of both Hudson's and Ayres'. It was an interesting theory. He'd have to think about it.

Meanwhile, here was his own daughter thigh-deep in little undershirts and booties, already warehousing for her own babies. Man, what was it with these women?

It was all Catherine Nicholson's fault. He shook his head. It was bad enough he was spending his day at the mall. No way was he going to sink even lower and spend it wallowing in baby things. "Ready to go?" he asked, and his steely voice dared them to say no.

Catherine sighed and glanced longingly at the boxes she hadn't had the chance to sort through. She knew she'd tested Jason's patience long enough. Men didn't like to sit around and wait much. As a group, they seemed on the hyperactive side to Catherine. They couldn't even sit still to watch television. No, they restlessly channel surfed the entire time. It was enough to make you nuts.

She gathered up her precious finds and rose from her cross-legged position on the floor. "The girls and I found some great stuff," she informed him happily. Catherine pointed to a nursery changing table that sat along one wall of the church's gathering space. "Think we could fit that into your trunk?" she asked. "It's only ten bucks. I can sell it for thirty once I clean it up a little."

Jason gritted his teeth. His new next-door neighbor's baby fixation was nothing to him. Absolutely nothing. She could buy two, three—heck *ten* of every baby product known to mankind—and it wouldn't affect him in the least because neither Catherine Nicholson nor any woman who shopped in her store would be shopping for any baby of his. Not in this lifetime.

It cost him, but he managed to say, "Sure. We'll get it in somehow."

Catherine beamed up at him. "Thanks."

Her smile almost undid him, but he remained strong. He had to. And he intended to have a talk with Maura that very night. Babies did more than smile and coo, although Maura had certainly been adorable when she'd done that. She needed to know some of the downside. "No problem," he said and, frustration giving him the strength of ten, he picked up the changing table with one hand and carried it to the pay table at the front of the church hall.

Catherine payed for her purchases and the girls' doll things as well. "It's your bonus for helping me look," she told them. They piled back into the car and, true to his word, Jason squeezed the changing table in.

He thought about rigging up some kind of blinders for her side of the car, but thankfully they passed no other rummage sale signs and the remainder of the trip to the mall was accomplished without further detour. It was with a sigh of relief that he pulled into a spot close to an entranceway and escorted the three women into the mall. "Where do you want to go first?" he asked, determined to be gracious and provide a nice day for his daughter. He knew it had been tough for her to capitulate and let him chaperon today.

Maura looked at Amy.

Amy looked back at Maura.

They both looked at Catherine.

Jason knew he was in trouble.

"Uh, well to tell you the truth, Mr. Engel—"

"We need to go to the bathroom," Maura broke in. "All that orange juice you made me drink at breakfast, you know."

"Yeah," Amy agreed brightly, although she hadn't had any orange juice at all. "We need to go to the bathroom. You and Aunt Cath can wait on that bench right there and talk. We'll be back in just a couple of minutes."

Both girls shot Catherine a pleading look.

She was sunk and she knew it. "All right. We'll wait right here and I'll—talk to Jason. If anybody acts weird in there or even looks at you crooked, you come right out, you hear me? Or scream. From here, we'll hear you."

Both girls looked thoroughly disgusted. "As if. Nobody's going to bother us in the bathroom," they informed Catherine condescendingly. "Sheesh."

"Just do it," Catherine instructed darkly.

"Okay, fine, have it your way," Amy said. "Anybody looks at us crooked, we'll yell bloody murder."

"Good. Now get out of here, creeps, while I talk to Maura's dad."

"We're going, we're going." And they went.

Catherine sat down on the bench and looked up at Jason. He studied her suspiciously for a moment or two before sitting next to her. "What are those two cooking up?" he asked.

Catherine sighed and began her explanation of Maura's budding breasts, for which she'd had to take Amy's word that they were blooming somewhere underneath the oversize sweatshirts both girls favored.

"She gets made fun of a lot by some girls who think they're cool, but are really jerks."

She'd pinkened noticeably from the effort of explaining the preteen facts of life to a virile man like

Jason when the girls returned, gazing at her with decidedly hopeful expressions.

Catherine took a quick peek at Jason to see how he was taking things.

The glower he wore was *not* encouraging.

"You two girls go on into the preteen section at Hudson's," she instructed. "They have—you know—there. Try on a few different styles. I'll be there in a few minutes to help and pay."

The girls took off like prisoners given a reprieve, leaving Catherine alone again with Jason.

"Don't go anywhere else," Catherine called after them. "I'll murder both of you if I have to go searching for you."

She decided to cut to the chase. Jason's narrowed eyes and tightly clamped lips were beginning to get to her. Nerves had her shifting positions on the bench. "So, anyway, the long and the short of it is, Maura needs new, um, underthings and was too embarrassed to tell you."

Catherine smiled hopefully in Jason's direction, wanting nothing more than for him to hand her his credit card so she could run into Hudson's and pay for Maura's bras and have this whole ridiculous episode behind her. Honestly, imagine a woman her age turning pink because she had to discuss underwear with a man.

Jason, unfortunately, did not appear ready to hand over the charge card and be done with things. No, he was turning a rather alarming shade of red, and she just knew he was going to have to blow off a little steam over the general meanness of junior-high girls. Catherine cringed and hung on to the edge of the mall bench when Jason jumped off his seat and began to pace in front of her. She had a feeling things were about to get rocky.

"I cannot believe," he got out between clenched teeth, "that my daughter would prefer to take verbal abuse from a bunch of prepubescent little witches rather than coming to me and letting me know what the problem is. I'd have bought her a damn brassiere. Hell, I'd have bought her a dozen. But does she come to me, her own father? Oh, no. She goes to a total stranger! How does she think that makes me feel? Sometimes I wonder if she even realizes I'm human. Heck, even if I were *subhuman*—which being a parent I'm sure is exactly how I'm categorized—I'd still be entitled to at least a few of the more *primitive* emotions, wouldn't I? Does she ever think about that at all? That I need to know I've taken care of her to the best of my ability? How can I do that if she doesn't talk to me? Answer me that."

"Ah, maybe I should run in and see what the girls are up to. I'll just pay for Maura's things and you can reimburse me later, how does that sound?"

Jason stopped right in front of Catherine and glared at her. She pulled her legs in and generally drew the rest of her body against the bench back in a physical and emotional retreat from what she saw in Jason's eyes. Mayhem, his eyes promised. Mayhem, murder and worse.

"What do I look like," Jason asked her, "some kind of maniac who'd turn violent at the mention of women's underwear?"

Catherine assumed the question was rhetorical.

Jason raked a hand through his hair in a gesture of

sheer frustration. "Man, I feel like a jerk. A total failure as a father. But how was I supposed to know she was—" he gestured at Catherine's chest "—doing that? Am I supposed to be able to read minds?"

"Uh—"

Jason waved his hand in the air. "Ah, none of this is your fault. I don't know why I'm yelling at you. I just get so darn frustrated sometimes—"

"Jason? The girls? We don't want to leave them on their own for too long."

"What? Oh, right." He leaned down and pulled her to him. "God only knows what they could get into. I can't wait for her to get out of this stage. Well, come on, let's go buy my daughter some bras." He snorted. "Like I almost know what I'm doing."

"The saleslady will help," Catherine assured him, having to practically skip to keep up with him. "But the thing is, maybe you should kind of stay back a bit until we get this taken care of. Maura might be more comfortable—"

"Damn," he muttered. "This is ridiculous. A girl needs a mother. Why couldn't she have been a boy? Buying a jockstrap would be a piece of cake compared to all this running around and hiding behind pillars while somebody else buys my daughter underwear."

Goodness, she'd set him off again. But, truthfully, she did feel kind of sorry for him. For both of them.

Poor Maura.

Poor Jason.

Poor Catherine, caught in the middle.

"I'd lay down my life for that child, Catherine, honest to God, I would."

She'd figured that much out for herself. "I know, Jason."

"She's gotten a raw deal all the way around. I'm doing my damnedest, but somehow it never seems to be enough. Okay, so how many of these things do we buy Maura? A reasonable number. I never could figure out why my former wife needed so many brassieres. There must have been at least two dozen floating around the place. You practically had to fight your way into the bedroom. I mean, you can only wear one at a time, right?"

"Uh, right."

"So all a person would need is two, right? One to wear while the other's in the wash. So maybe we should buy three and be safe all around, huh?"

"Uh—" Catherine thought about the colorful assortment in her own drawers. She enjoyed pretty underthings.

Resolutely she turned her head away from the lingerie display in the window of the specialty store they were walking by, even though the pale blue lacy bra and matching panties over on the far left were calling her name. Catherine could hear them, quite distinctly.

But no, she'd be strong. She had a dozen perfectly good, more-than-adequate sets at home. Evidently, that was ten more than she needed.

She talked Jason into four preteen brassieres for Maura. He grumbled, but reached for his wallet so Catherine could run back and pay for Maura's selections.

"They were $13.50 apiece?" he complained. "That's crazy. I wouldn't pay more than six bucks for a pair of boxer shorts."

"It's not quite the same thing," Catherine assured him, as she impatiently waited for him to find the right card. "I paid $28.00 for my last bra."

That was meant to reassure him of the reasonableness of his purchase, but instead, his head reared up, charge cards forgotten as he studied first her face, then let his eyes drop to examine her chest with a great deal more interest than he'd displayed up until then. "I'd like to see that," he said.

His eyes were narrowed, as though intense concentration would allow him to see through her top, and Catherine suddenly felt quite naked. She shivered and fought the urge to fold her arms over her breasts. "I haven't got that one on today," she explained carefully, all but grabbing the bit of plastic he finally held out. "The one I'm wearing right now was only $18." Good grief, how had they gotten onto the subject of her underwear? She should have known better than to agree to help Maura and Amy. Next time she would know better.

Catherine turned and walked back to the counter where Maura and Amy waited huddled over their purchase in a protective stance designed to keep any of the myriad anonymous shoppers swirling around the salesclerk's island from realizing what they were buying. Jason's speculative stare burned a hole in her back the entire way.

Jason had difficulty concentrating the rest of the day. All he could think about was a twenty-eight-dollar brassiere. Had to be silk or some other smooth, satiny fabric like that, he figured. Red? No, black. He narrowed his eyes as he considered that.

Catherine hadn't dressed to entice. She wore jeans

with a sweater. The collar of a shirt curved down neatly over the neckline of the sweater. The jeans were faded, but the sweater was knit in bright fall colors. Full-hued reds, oranges and yellows. The blouse was a crisp white with a small embroidered fall leaf in the point of each collar.

It was a bold combination, at least from the waist up.

Mightn't a person, a woman who favored such full-bodied coloration on the outside extend a similar boldness to her choice of undergarments?

Her bra could be black.

It could even be one of those demi-cup things that did nothing but hold a woman's breast up like some kind of offering that begged a man to touch it.

Jason ran a finger around the neckline of his own battleship gray sweatshirt, feeling suddenly over-heated. From his position at the entrance to the pre-teen section, he could see Catherine smiling and talk-ing in an animated fashion to the salesclerk as she signed the sales slip and took back his credit card. *His* credit card. The fact that it *was* his spoke of an intimacy that made him both uneasy and, he had to face it, excited. He watched the saleslady slip fifty-four dollars' worth of underwear—which nobody in the world would ever see but a couple of snot-faced locker-room preadolescents, who wouldn't appreciate them, anyway—into a bag and hand it to Catherine.

Jason watched as the three females turned away from the counter and headed his way. Catherine had already removed her jacket. She held it over one arm. Maybe she'd get even warmer and remove her sweater? A guy could hope. Her blouse was white. Surely you'd be able to see black through that.

He shook his head to clear it. Good grief, what was wrong with him? His daughter was only a few feet away, and here he was acting like a sixteen-year-old. He'd better not catch any jerk-faced high school jock with thoughts like his written on his face. He'd kill him.

"Dad?"

"Hmm?" He looked down. Maura and Amy were right in front of him giving him a curious look.

"I said we were ready to go."

"Oh. Oh, well lead on, then."

Catherine handed the bag she'd carried to Maura. "No one knows what's in here now. It's okay for you to carry it." She put her hand on Maura's shoulder. "Don't you have something to say to your father?"

Maura studied the carpeting at her feet and rolled the top of the paper bag shut a few extra folds. "Thanks, Dad," she mumbled and turned pink. "I appreciate this."

All of Jason's frustrations fled, and he gave his daughter's shoulders a light squeeze, knowing anything more done in public would only pinken her further. Heck, the brief touch was probably pushing his luck.

It was scary how much he loved this child of his. Crazy as she made him, he sometimes ached just looking at her, she was so beautiful to him. And he'd be perfectly happy to personally wring the necks of those girls who'd given her a hard time in the gym locker room.

"You're welcome, honey." He put a finger under

her chin and gently tilted it up so he could see her face. "Next time, come to me, okay? It almost killed me to know you were getting grief at school just because you didn't think you could talk to me about female stuff. I know it's hard, but all we've got is each other. Let me help you, all right?"

Maura gave a brief nod, and Jason knew that was all he was going to get. "Do you want me to carry that for you?" He nodded at the bag she held.

Maura looked scandalized. "No, Dad, it's—"

Jason rolled his eyes and pulled her under his arm as they started to walk out of the store. "I know what it is, and last time I checked they didn't bite. Real men aren't afraid to take one on." Oh, God. Jason swallowed. Catherine's twenty-eight-dollar one, scratch that, her *eighteen*-dollar one scared him half to death. He'd been fixating on it back there, he knew he had, and it had been one heck of a long time since he'd had those kinds of feelings.

Jason cleared his throat. "Now why don't you hand over that bag so your hands will be free for whatever other trouble you and Amy decide to get into?"

Jason looked over at Catherine who was smiling at him. Was it only women who had hot flashes? He'd swear he was having one right then. "Warm in here, isn't it? I'd love to peel my sweatshirt off, but I didn't think to put a shirt on underneath it."

"You're hot?" Catherine asked, surprised. For her, it was constitutionally impossible to be hot from November 1 through about the middle of May. With enough layers, she usually managed tepid, occasionally pushed it to warm, but she was never hot. "That's too bad. I'm almost always on the cold side, so I'm fine.'' At least she had been until Jason had mentioned he wasn't wearing so much as an undershirt. He had the sleeves of that old gray sweatshirt pushed up, and the tops of his forearms were covered with crisp black hair. Did a similar mat blanket his chest? Could she convince Jason that no one in the mall would mind if he took off his sweatshirt and shopped bare-chested so she could find out? Good grief, she was losing her mind. Just thinking about it had her body temperature on the rise. How strange.

"Where to?" Jason asked his small gaggle. She wasn't even slightly warm? Well, damn. He hated to suffer this insanity all by himself. Misery loved company and all of that. And just thinking about that twenty-eight-dollar brassiere was driving his blood pressure up into stroke territory.

They spent quite awhile in an earring boutique, only leaving when Jason threatened to get his nose pierced. He offered to treat them all to lunch, but Catherine insisted on paying for Amy and herself.

"No, this is fair," she told him when he tried to pick up the entire tab. "I had planned on taking Amy out today, anyway. There's no reason for you to pay for the two of us."

She was right, there wasn't. Somehow, the relief he should have felt was missing. Instead, Jason was ticked that he had no claim on her, no valid reason to insist on paying for her food. Catherine brought out the caveman in him. Next thing you knew, he'd want to be responsible for her shelter as well. Good grief. Talk about your perverse male psyche, man, his was going to run him ragged by the end of the day.

"I'm grateful for the way you helped out this

morning," he told her grumpily, not sounding the least bit grateful. "You were a big help. That's reason enough."

"No it's not," she insisted, wondering why he sounded irritated. Why, he ought to be grateful she wasn't allowing him to pick up the tab. Possibly he was just putting up a polite argument before happily capitulating? He was a man, who knew? The few dates she'd had, she'd paid her own way. Catherine didn't want anybody getting the idea she owed them anything. Especially now when she'd given up on finding Mr. Right or even Mr. Sort of Right. Now she just wanted Mr. Anonymous Donor. She put down her ten-dollar bill next to Jason's and walked away from the cashier.

Jason took his change and followed the women out into the mall again, scowling.

Catherine fanned her face with her hand. The restaurant had been warm. Sitting in that tight booth with Amy's warm little body right next to hers, and having Jason Engel's incredible masculine form sprawled just across from her had made it all the warmer. She needed to take her sweater off for a while.

Jason's eyes just about dropped out of their sockets when Catherine whipped it off over her head and tied it around her waist. Then they almost crossed before he realized what he was doing, and looked determinedly away. He did not care *what* the woman wore beneath that crisp white blouse of hers. No, he did not.

But he thought he'd seen a hint of black.

Even the thought of it had him staggering for a step or two. Man alive, there was something strange going on here, and he needed to find out what it was and counteract it before he was reduced to crawling after the woman on his hands and knees and babbling like an idiot.

He stiffened his knees, forced his legs to move and caught up with her.

At the touch of his hand on her arm, Catherine turned and looked up at him, her surprise evident. "Jason?" she asked.

"Listen, Catherine, I've just remembered something. When we're done here for the day, we're to drop the girls off at Amy's house. Her mother called right before I picked you up and said she'd be happy to take them for a while this evening. There's some kind of mousetrap car they have to make for science class. It has to travel fifteen feet for an A. She thought they could get started on it. Maura seemed kind of excited, and your sister said she'd pick up some mousetraps for them to experiment on while she was out running errands today.

"You've saved my daughter from taking a lot more grief at the hands of those other girls, and her lunkhead father is grateful. I think we ought to take your sister up on her offer. I'd like to take you out to dinner tonight." He'd spend an evening with Catherine, undistracted by his daughter, so he could concentrate on Catherine's strange allure. Then he'd figure out the antidote.

"But the girls—"

"Will have a ball. Look at them. They're not sick of each other's company yet."

Monica could care less about building a mousetrap car for Amy, Catherine knew. Her sister was scheming. She ought to say no. But, heck, what would she do if she stayed home, wash her hair again? "Okay," she said instead. "It sounds like fun."

Jason stayed by her side the rest of the afternoon, taking her arm to guide her through crowds and touching Catherine unnecessarily at other times, leaving her to wonder what in the world had come over him. Had the restaurant where they'd eaten put some strange spice in his soup or what?

Chapter Five

Jason dropped Catherine and Amy off around three o'clock. Amy called her mother for permission to stay at Maura's until it was time for Jason to take the girls to Monica's, then took off like a shot when permission was granted. Catherine tried to shrug it off. So much for her kid fix. She told herself that Amy was simply getting to that age where she was going to prefer the company of her own peer group. Informing herself she'd be an idiot to take it personally helped, but only marginally. Finally Catherine, feeling both pitiful and put-upon, went off to the paint store all by her lonesome, determined to at least get the supplies for painting the nursery that day. That way she'd have accomplished something toward achieving her goal.

Catherine took one of every yellow paint chip on the rack. The store she'd chosen to haunt carried three different brands of base, so it amounted to quite a handful of minimally different yellows for her to

study. She carried them over to the windows and examined them in natural light. She brought them deep
into the back of the store to see what artificial lighting
did to them.

"This one's too deep," she murmured to herself
and eliminated a deep gold chip.

"This one's almost neon. It looks like it would
glow in the dark." That one followed the first. "This
is the nineties, not the seventies."

She examined a third. "Too bold," she decided.
"Don't want to blind the poor little thing." Moving
back to the windows, she declared a fourth out of the
running. "Almost electric looking. What baby could
fall asleep surrounded by walls this color? Babies
need a soft color, a soothing color to calm them down
when they've got colic."

"Doing a nursery?" the store clerk asked from
somewhere behind her.

Catherine looked up from her perusal of the color
cards in her hand. What had seemed so real and def-
inite when talking with Monica seemed almost out of
focus now after spending most of her day with Jason
and Maura.

Why *did* she want a baby so badly?

She had to think about her response, but once she
had, Catherine's answer was firm. "Yes," she declared. "I'm doing a nursery. The end of the crib has
darling twin brown bears on it. One's wearing a yellow sweater and his sister's got a little yellow dress
on, so I'm considering one of these." She indicated
the remaining samples.

"Ah," the clerk said. "Yellow's always cheerful,

isn't it?" she asked. "And so neutral. It's appropriate for a boy or girl."

"Right. Just what I was thinking," Catherine said. "I've managed to narrow it down some, but I'm having trouble choosing from what I've got left here."

"Do you have a sample of the curtain fabric with you?"

"Uh, no. I guess I figured I'd do the walls first, then work around them." She hadn't thought any such thing. Catherine had simply never gone so far as to actually ready a nursery for her dream baby before and so had no real clue exactly how to do it. And she wasn't about to admit to the clerk she was contemplating decorating a room for a child who existed only in her deepest longings.

The clerk was nodding agreeably, unaware of Catherine's inner turmoil. "Uh-huh, uh-huh. Well, I've got an idea if you're interested."

"Hmm? Oh, sure. I guess so."

"Take all three."

"Excuse me?"

"Make it easy on yourself. I'll give you three different yellows all from the same family. Paint the walls the deepest one first. You'll hate it. Looks like an overdone Easter egg."

Catherine blinked. "Then why would I do it?"

"Because," the woman paused dramatically, "I'm also going to give you some literature on rag rolling. The first stage always looks bad, but you've got to force yourself to keep going. Here's what you do next, you rag the two lighter shades over that base coat, cut the trim out in almost a pure white with maybe just a dollup of yellow in it, maybe put white lace curtains in the windows and you've got walls with some depth to them and a nursery with real class. A little more work, but well worth the effort,'' the clerk declared authoritatively.

"I see," Catherine said, though truthfully, she was having trouble visualizing how this was all going to come together. But the woman seemed so sure. "Um, okay. I'll try it," she decided. "Why not? If I hate it, I can always paint over it." God knew there was no hurry to get the room done, not if she didn't get up the courage to talk to her ob sometime soon.

"That's the spirit," the clerk said approvingly. "Give it a go. And I promise you won't need or want to paint over it. You're going to love the finished product.''

Catherine left the store, her arms laden with a gallon of base, several quarts for ragging and trim work, brushes, drop cloths, paint cleaner and a slew of other items the salesclerk had deemed necessary for her project. Catherine wondered if she worked on commission.

She put her supplies up in the spare bedroom, refusing to think any further on the why of her need to do this, then went to shower in preparation for her "date." As she ran the soap down one arm and up the other, Catherine contemplated the puzzle that was Jason Engel.

Why had he suddenly decided to take her out to dinner?

He'd certainly kept his distance most of the morning. Then suddenly, shortly after lunch, there'd been some kind of major turnaround. What?

Catherine rinsed her arms, then faced the spray of

water cascading down from the showerhead. Funny, her chest had never been that sensitive to the pounding water before. Catherine picked up the soap and washed her breasts. Good grief, what was happening to her? She looked down at herself, taking in the way her nipples had immediately beaded up from her own touch. And sensitive? Holy cow. There was also a tightening of something or another down at the junction of her legs that was new as well.

Concentrating, Catherine could only come up with one difference. She'd never had Jason Engel on her mind when showering before.

But this was bad, Catherine told herself as she quickly finished up her shower. She could barely stand to dry herself, her skin was so sensitized. *Stop it,* she lectured herself. She was done with men. Through, Catherine forcibly reminded herself. Jason was a neighbor, nothing more. She'd be friendly to him so he'd let her borrow Maura. Maybe he'd even let Maura baby-sit once she had her baby, although it was more likely he'd stop her visits altogether. It was so unfair that people could be so narrow-minded about things like this, but she'd bet a day's profit at Hand Arounds that Jason Engel would prove to be just that.

Catherine gave a heartfelt sigh.

The doorbell rang as she secured her second earring. With a last look in the mirror, Catherine went to answer it.

"Hi," she said, then grimaced a bit at the slightly breathy tone she heard in her voice. Hopefully Jason hadn't noticed. But the man looked good, very good. He'd probably make any member of the opposite sex

have to monitor their breathing a little bit. Catherine
needed to believe that.

"Hi," Jason said with a smile. "You look nice."
Oh, man, he thought, cringing inside himself. You are
out of practice, Engel. You look nice? If that's as
smooth as you get, you are in deep trouble, old man.

Calm down, he told himself. So it had been awhile.
He'd get better. And besides, the sight of Catherine
in her soft blouse and swirly skirt was enough to
tongue-tie anybody, he assured himself. "You, um,
ready to go?"

"Just let me grab my purse and a jacket and I'll
be right with you," she assured him. "Do you want
to come in for a minute?"

Jason stepped forward, eager to get away from the
prying eyes he felt burning into his back. Maura and
Amy were gone. He'd dropped them off half an hour
ago, and he barely knew the other neighbors, but
damn it, it felt like the whole world was watching
him make an idiot of himself. He felt conspicuous
and stupid out there in a way he never had before
when picking up a date. "Sure. Thanks." He came
into her small entrance foyer, closing the front door
behind him.

Catherine retrieved her jacket, but before she could
put it on, Jason took it and held it for her. She slid
her arms in easily. Jason was one of the few men
she'd run across who held a coat low enough so that
you didn't partially dislocate your arms or half stran-
gle yourself trying to get into it when they helped
you. "Thank you," she said.

"You're welcome," he replied, and with a flourish

he couldn't quite help at this small success, opened her door and ushered Catherine out into the night.

He drove downtown. South Bend was not a particularly large city, but it did boast some very nice places to eat. Jason picked the LaSalle Grill. The food was superb, and he wanted to put Catherine in as intimate an atmosphere as possible. See if he still felt the strange sizzle then. Jason saw to it that their table was off in a corner, and he seated Catherine with care, catching the scent of her light perfume as he did so. He took the chair directly across from her.

"All the years I've lived in this town, I've never been here," Catherine admitted, looking around.

"Then you're in for a real treat," Jason informed her. "The food here is excellent." He sat back in his chair and studied Catherine. In the glow of the table's candle, her eyes appeared a dark, deep chocolate, her skin seemed to become luminescent and her hair looked so soft in the candle's glow it was all he could do not to reach out and touch it for himself.

"Are you very hungry?" Jason asked, when he felt he'd got his control back.

"Not really. We had a late lunch, remember?"

"Okay, let's skip the appetizers then, because we'll want to save room for their desserts. But I have to tell you, it's been kind of a traumatic day for me. I don't know about you, but I could really use a glass of wine right about now."

Catherine curved her lips into an understanding smile.

"That sounds good," she agreed.

"Do you have any preference?"

"I could be happy with either red or white, but to

tell you the truth, on a chilly night like this I do lean more to red."

"Fine," Jason said and scanned the wine list. "How about a nice Merlot?"

"Perfect."

He signaled the waiter and placed the order.

A short time later, Jason had ordered aged steak for both of them, and they sat sipping their wine. Catherine checked the level in her cup. It was barely half-gone. How could her judgment already be impaired? And yet, she was pretty sure it was. How else could she explain her heightened awareness of the man sitting across from her? In twenty-seven years she'd been out on plenty of dates, but nothing like this had ever happened to her before.

She couldn't take her eyes off him. The room might as well be empty except for Jason Engel. She'd been exquisitely aware of his warmth when he'd stood next to her in the crowded waiting area, just as she'd been aware of the rightness in his protectiveness when he'd drawn her up close against him and out of harm's way as newcomers pushed through the crowded entrance to give their names to the hostess. His scent filled her nostrils even now; clean, woodsy but not at all overpowering. He smelled simply—male.

Jason shifted in his seat. This was not working. This evening out was supposed to thank Catherine for her helpfulness that day, get them both a really good meal neither had had any hand in preparing, and most importantly, remind Jason of the silliness of somebody his age, in his position, going through this ritual all over again when they should know better by now.

Unfortunately, right now all he could think about

was how when they'd been waiting to be seated, he'd realized she was just the right height for the top of her head to tuck perfectly under his chin.

He shook his head. How ridiculous.

"Jason?"

"Hmm?"

"Jason, does this wine seem kind of potent to you or is it just me?"

"What? The wine?" He frowned at his glass. "You don't like it? I can order you something else."

"No, it's good. I'm just wondering about the alcohol content."

"It doesn't seem particularly strong to me."

"Oh." Too bad. "I was just wondering." She would die a thousand deaths before admitting to Monica she felt any sort of attraction for Jason. But the conversation was kind of lagging because she was just so darn aware of him that she was tongue-tied.

Catherine almost kissed the waiter, she was so grateful when the food came.

Jason waited until they'd been served, then gave Catherine what he hoped would pass as a smile. "So, Catherine, tell me about yourself. You certainly seem to have a knack with the preadolescent crowd. I sure appreciate everything you did today."

"Oh, well, you're welcome. It was no problem." Catherine shrugged. "To tell you the truth, I really enjoy kids, and Maura is just so typical for her age I have to laugh."

Jason snorted. "Easy for you to say. You don't have to live with it."

Catherine reached over and and touched his hand in a sympathetic gesture. "I know. It must be hard for you all by yourself. Listen, anytime you want, I'd be happy to help out. Just say the word. Maura's a neat kid." Catherine looked at her lap. "I always wanted to have a family of my own. This may be as close as I get, so don't hesitate to call. I'll actually be grateful."

"If that's what you want, why haven't you gotten married and had your own kids?" Jason asked, knowing it was none of his business but inexplicably interested in everything about this attractive woman across from him.

Catherine shrugged. "It just never happened."

"I can't believe there was a lack of interested men. You're a beautiful woman inside and out. Warm, giving. There must have been somebody."

Catherine shook her head while she blushed. "No. I mean, yes, there have been guys, but never that special feeling, that spark, you know? My sister tells me I'm too picky. Maybe she's right. My head knows Cinderella already got Prince Charming, but my heart still believes in fairy tales. It's still waiting."

Jason looked at the tabletop to where Catherine's hand still covered his. That special feeling? That spark? He wondered if she felt the slight sizzle he did where their hands met. Far be it from him to point it out. He slid his hand out from under hers and tried to make his release appear nonchalant by using that hand to pick up his water goblet. He cleared his throat. "Well, so, how's your steak? Tender enough?"

"It's fine," Catherine said, immediately recognizing the male discomfort with any topic halfway intimate. "I can cut it with my fork. And I meant what

I said. I'll take Maura anytime you want. In fact, if it will make you feel better, I'll ask for the first favor. I'm going to start painting one of the upstairs rooms tomorrow, probably as soon as I get home from church. You wouldn't happen to have a stepladder I could borrow, would you?''

Jason swallowed a bite of potato, irritated with the way his hand felt so cold and empty now. "Sure," he said. "Give me a call when you're ready. I'll bring it over."

"That's all right. I'll come get it."

Jason frowned. "Catherine, I'm not letting you lug that thing back and forth when I'll be home, anyway. It's big, it's awkward, and it's heavy. You might hurt yourself. I'll do it."

Wasn't that sweet? Jason Engel really was a nice man, Catherine thought. Monica just might be right, after all. Oh, not the getting married part, but maybe, just maybe it would be better to have someone you knew and liked, someone you trusted to father your baby. That way you knew more what you'd be getting into. After all, what if the anonymous donor turned out to be a psychopathic killer? Your child would have half psycho genes. But someone warm and loving, someone like Jason Engel, why he'd pass on warm, loving characteristics to a child.

Catherine gnawed her lower lip. It was something to think about.

Jason watched Catherine chew her lip. He found it fascinating the way she sucked that pouty bottom lip in and worked her upper teeth over it. He had to remind himself to exhale.

Jason picked up his fork and put his attention to

his food. The quicker they ate, the sooner they'd be out of there.

He cleared his plate quickly. Catherine felt the change in his attitude and tried not to dawdle, but there was no way to keep up with Jason. The man had practically inhaled his steak and broccoli. His huge baked potato was nothing but a distant fond memory, as well. Catherine made what she felt was a valiant effort, but it amounted to nothing more than a dent in the food on her plate by the time Jason had finished. Now he sat across the small table, and his eyes followed her fork from her plate to her mouth and back again.

She managed two more bites, but ended up setting her fork down. "Jason, I can't eat if you're going to stare at me like that."

Jason's eyes rose from her mouth to meet her discomfited gaze. "What?"

Catherine pursed her lips and studied him a bit while she tried to figure out what she'd done or said to make the evening turn weird. Maybe she shouldn't have admitted she'd wanted to get married and have children. In her shop she dealt mostly with women, and she was used to being more up-front. But if she'd freaked him out, that wouldn't explain the heat in his gaze that warmed her and had her on edge. Jason was studying her like a predator sizing up his prey. Frankly, Catherine felt like she was about to be mauled at any minute. She shook her head. That was crazy. Jason Engel didn't want her, he was simply grateful for the way she'd taken over getting his daughter the bras she'd needed.

Wasn't he?

Of course he was.

Catherine picked up her fork, took another look at Jason and set it back down. "I can't do it."

Jason didn't protest. He quickly signaled the waiter. "I'll have it packed for you, okay? You might want to eat it later."

"All right." She was no good at this dating stuff. Obviously she'd misinterpreted his earlier looks. Now he was acting as though he couldn't wait to get rid of her.

He ordered two crème caramel deserts to be packed as well. "We'll have them with some coffee at my house. These are too good to pass up. They're drizzled with burned sugar and absolutely out of this world. By the time we get back, you'll probably have room."

"Probably. I guess." Catherine was totally thrown for a loop. He didn't want to get rid of her? Then why had he been in such an all-fired rush? They waited for Jason's charge receipt, then she followed him through the restaurant and out the door.

"Jason, is something wrong?" Catherine finally asked when they were in the car and headed for home. "Your mind seems to be elsewhere."

"What? Oh, no, not at all." Jason patted the deserts on the seat between them. "Just looking forward to dessert." Hopefully, there'd be a little more to it than just the crème caramel, although he wasn't about to admit any such thing to Catherine. She'd find out soon enough. He pushed his foot slightly harder on the gas pedal. His heart was going to explode in his chest if he didn't get his arms around her and kiss her soon.

Jason kept his hands on the steering wheel as he drove home, but it took concentration. His shoulders were stiff with the effort he'd had to exert when he pulled into his driveway.

"Do you want to go get Maura before we go in? Then you wouldn't have to go back out in the cold and you could put your car away for the night."

No way. An hour or so from now would do just fine. Jason glanced at the dashboard, its dials glowing green in the evening dark. "It's only eight-thirty," he said. "Maura and Amy will want more time together. I'll get her in a while. I'm enjoying this little bit of non-business-related adult companionship, to tell you the truth."

A compliment? Catherine flushed there in the dark. Imagine getting flustered at her age by such a vague remark as that. This was all Monica's fault for putting ideas into her head. Oh, well, might as well see the evening through. "We could go to my place," Catherine heard herself say. "I just bought some coffee. It's still out on the countertop."

"All right." Jason got out, rounded the car and opened the door for her. He walked her to her front door, then waited while she unlocked it. He followed her into the small entranceway.

Catherine stood in the foyer and tried to breathe. The hallway was too small. He was too close. That nearness made her distracted. "Let me take your coat," she offered a bit desperately. "And then we can go back to the kitchen."

Instead of handing Catherine his jacket, Jason helped her remove her own. He waited while she hung it up, only then giving her his.

She hoped her shiver when he'd accidentally touched her hadn't communicated itself to him. "That takes care of that," Catherine said brightly. "Let's get that coffee percolating."

Jason had been enjoying the close confines of the entranceway. He'd been losing himself in trying to identify the scent of Catherine's shampoo. Peaches. Maybe apples. Whatever, it was delicious and certainly giving him an appetite. "Sure. Whatever you say."

Catherine hit the kitchen light switch and Jason almost staggered as he took in his surroundings. His hand flew to his chest, shocked by what he was seeing. "What the hell is all this?" he said, staring in amazement all around him.

"What's all of what?" Catherine asked, looking over her shoulder.

Words failed him. Thought failed him. Jason was reduced to stuttering. He pointed at the kitchen table and nearby countertops. "Th-that."

Catherine's head swung back around to try and see what Jason was so visibly shaken by. Her eyes widened when she realized what the problem was. "Those are baby things," she explained, quite sure Jason was capable of identifying them himself. "The mother of triplets came in yesterday and left me everything the boys had grown out of, which amounted to quite a bit. The store was busy all day yesterday, so I brought them home to sort through and decide what I wanted to buy so I didn't have to go in on my day off."

Jason supported himself with one hand on a countertop. His heart was still not fully recovered from being taken by surprise with all this—nursery stuff. The rummage sale had been one thing. He'd had some warning. Catherine hadn't bought all that much, and she'd made it clear it was for her store. Baby business dealings. Yes, *that* he could handle. But the sheer quantity of small-size things here was mind-boggling. "What's the difference? It's still work, isn't it?" Say yes, he silently implored. His libido was fading quickly in the face of all this baby paraphernalia. Nothing like a stack of diapers to cool a man's lust.

Catherine smiled fondly at a small tower of pastel receiving blankets. "This is the fun part of my job. Oohing and aahing over all the cute baby things."

Jason barely prevented his eyes from rolling back in his head. "Oh, God," he said. "Where's the coffeemaker? Maybe we could take our dessert into the living room to eat. Would that be okay?" He had to get out of there before he hyperventilated.

"Sure. I guess. The coffeemaker's right there." She pointed to a corner of the countertop.

Jason nodded. "Good. Hurry. Let's get it made."

Men were weird. Every one of them, Catherine decided as she watched him from the corner of her eye. She filled the pot with water and put it in the machine. "There. Relax. It's perking. Caffeine is on the way. You want any cream or sugar?"

"A little bit of milk. No sugar. How about some plates for the desserts?"

"Up there." Catherine indicated an upper cabinet.

"Got 'em. I'll carry these into the living room and wait for you there, okay?"

"Yeah, sure."

Catherine watched Jason exit the kitchen as fast as his legs would carry him.

Chapter Six

Catherine brought mugs of coffee and spoons into the living room a few minutes later. Jason sat sprawled on her sofa, looking frazzled. "Jason, what in the world is the matter with you? I hate to say it, but you're acting very strange all of a sudden."

"Sorry," he said, closing his eyes briefly. "It was all that baby stuff in the kitchen. Caught me by surprise. Any man would have had heart palpitations walking into that amount of little kid stuff. Believe me, Sylvester Stallone would have had problems in there. Arnold Schwarzenegger—"

"All right, all right. I get the idea." Catherine put the mugs down on the small coffee table in front of the sofa, then positioned herself in the wing chair next to it. She took a sip of the fragrant coffee. "Why?" she asked.

Jason sat up and lifted his own mug. He shrugged. "I don't know. I think it's a male thing. We're more into the planning and production end of the business. Final product is more a woman's domain, I guess.''

How silly. Catherine picked up her spoon and ate a bite of dessert while she thought. "Mmm, this is good," she said, savoring the delicate flavors. Then she looked right at him. "What about Maura? You can't sit there and tell me she gives you the willies. You love her. It's as obvious as the nose on your face.''

Jason reached up and felt his face. "You don't like my nose?''

Catherine sighed. "Oh, stop. You know what I meant."

Jason heaved a giant sigh himself. "Yeah, I do. I think it's another guy thing. We're not comfortable discussing emotions. Of course I love Maura, although to tell you the truth she can give me the chills with some of this adolescent testing she's going in for lately. Still, she's flesh of my flesh, blood of my blood, bone of—''

Catherine gave him a disgusted glance. "All right, already. Stop."

Jason shrugged. "Yeah, I love her. I loved her as a baby, when she carried on over cutting a tooth, and I love her now, when she's carrying on over developing a bosom. There, are you happy? I admitted it.''

"Then why do a few sets of sleepers make you break out in goose bumps?" Catherine asked, needing to understand and cursing Monica because of that need.

Jason shoveled in several large scoops of crème caramel without tasting it. "Partially it was the sheer quantity out there. Raising one kid is tough enough.

Trying to bring up an entire slew—I don't even want to think about it.'' He looked at his plate, surprised to find half of his dessert gone.

"But more than that, it's that I guess I've learned from bitter experience that babies can't be undone. You can't return them when things go sour.''

Catherine's eyes widened. "What are you talking about?''

Jason shrugged. "Having Maura was a great experience. I won't pretend I didn't try talking my ex-wife into waiting a bit longer. I didn't think we were ready. But once she was pregnant, I loved watching her body ripen with my child. I went to those classes with her where they teach you to breathe like a demented idiot and lie on tennis balls.'' He snorted. "I was there when she was born. The doctor let me cut the umbilical cord. I get all choked up just thinking about it.''

Catherine was getting a little teary-eyed just listening.

"Karen wanted that baby more than anything, but I guess she didn't find motherhood as fulfilling as she thought it would be. After a couple of years she was discontent. You could see it in her face. She went back to work when Maura was three. I changed jobs so I could be around more. That's when I started doing house mortgage appraisals for banks. All I have to do is go out and inspect the property they're considering loaning money on. I can do the comparables and the rest of the figuring at home on my computer.''

"So that's why you're able to be around so much.''

"Yeah. Anyway, we limped along for a while like that, but I knew our relationship was suffering. Going back to work was just putting a Band-Aid on a deeper hurt. Basically, we just didn't love each other any more. It was a gradual thing, there was no single moment you could put your finger on as the turning point. Eventually Karen applied for a divorce. I didn't fight for Maura because I thought a girl needed her mother. Karen had other ideas. When she got remarried, she wanted to put everything behind her. But you can't do that. Maura can't get unborn and I wouldn't let her even if she could. I love her so much that sometimes it's like an ache in my gut. I can't stand to see her hurt. It rips me apart to have Karen ignoring her now. Maura didn't do anything to deserve that. She should have her mother available to take her bra shopping. Thank God you were willing and able. But I gotta tell you, all I have to do is look at all those little things out in the kitchen now and I get nothing but melancholy.''

Catherine felt pretty sad herself right then. She had a lot to think about. Jason was a man of complex parts. He felt deeply and had waded his way through a lot of pain to get to this point in his life.

"I'm sorry. I didn't mean to ramble on like that." Jason ran his hand through his hair, thoroughly mussing it up. "It's not your fault you make your living selling baby products. It's me. I just can't look at them without thinking about everything that can go wrong. They're so perfect when they're born. The quintessential blank slates. Then *we* get a hold of them."

Jason jumped up to pace. "The realities of parenting are just so different from the daydreams. Other people's children scream and get colic, yours won't.

Those other people simply didn't handle their children correctly. Yours will fall right into your game plan because you've read a book and will therefore do things correctly. You will have perfect control at all times. Of course, the clincher is that you and your spouse provided your offspring with superior genes. How can things go wrong?''

Jason paused and rubbed his hands over his eyes in a gesture that spoke more of mental fatigue than physical. ''Well let me tell you, I can't even begin to count the ways. You'd get dizzy if I tried to enumerate even half the ways a kid thinks to test you. I don't know where those textbook children and their perfect parents are hiding, but I'm here to tell you, if I ever meet one, I'll probably smack 'em. And I'm sure that's because I feel like such a failure as a parent. Maura deserves so much better. I want the best for her, but no matter how many books I read, I still seem to screw up at every turn. Today's another great example.''

''Jason, stop beating yourself up. You were terrific today.''

He sipped his coffee, then shook his head. ''No. Today she needed a mother. A woman she could talk to about woman things. No matter how hard I try I can't be that for her.'' Jason walked back to the side table, picked up his mug and took a sip. Briefly he contemplated Catherine over the rim. ''Once again, all I can say is thank God you were available. I'd have been sunk without you.''

Catherine pushed her mug aside and rose, too. ''You'd have managed.''

Jason shrugged. ''Maybe. More than likely she'd

have never 'fessed up to what was bothering her. I'd still be in the dark.'' He finished off his coffee and set the mug down. All this introspection had wreaked havoc on his libido. He no longer felt the need to jump her bones or die. Damn. ''I guess I'd better go make sure your sister's house is still standing,'' he said.

Catherine walked with him to the front door, relieved and disappointed to see the evening end. She had a lot of thinking to do.

Jason's hand fell companionably on her shoulder as they moved together. In the front hall, he turned Catherine to face him. ''I'm sorry for unloading on you,'' he said. His hand squeezed her shoulder. ''Ah, you never know. With any luck when you marry and have your children, maybe he or she *will* be perfect. I hope so, for you.''

Catherine managed a small grin, although she wasn't feeling all that lighthearted. Jason had no idea how near and dear to her heart this topic was. ''And if it's not, may I call you and whine?''·

Jason laughed. The low chuckles washed over Catherine, delighting her with their warmth.

''You can call and whine,'' he said. ''Just don't expect any real useful advice. Parenting, I've decided, is one of those sink or swim things. Every man for himself. Someday, you'll see.''

''Thanks a whole bunch.''

Jason laughed again and Catherine was immediately captivated by the rich sound. She smiled back, pleased with his release. Up until a few moments ago, she hadn't been sure he was capable of relaxing enough to enjoy himself. ''What's so funny?''

"I was just thinking about all those beautiful itsy-bitsy dresses with the fancy smocking on them that you bought today for your shop. We had a bunch like that for Maura. Ever wonder why they're still so perfect when they get to a rummage sale?"

Catherine's eyes narrowed suspiciously. "Why?"

"'Cuz a kid can't crawl in them. They get real frustrated when they try, to say nothing of the way their knees get all banged up. Maybe I ought to come into your shop and have a little talk with all those prospective parents. Let them know that if they're thinking about how darling their little one will look dressed in one of those, they can just forget it."

"Don't you dare."

He chuckled. "They need to know how perverse nature can be. Anyone buying one of those little dresses is obviously envisioning a feminine little flower. They'll get just the opposite. Trust me. That baby will grow up to be a tomboy. One who wouldn't be caught dead in one of those lacy pink bonnets with the long ribbon ties."

Catherine huffed. "You can't know that." A tomboy. Good grief. And here she'd set aside one of the sweetest little newborn bonnets, just in case. Why the brim had to be six inches, at least, and dripping with trim. Catherine knew it was stupid, but she had it upstairs in a box in the closet—for her own little flower of femininity when the time came.

He rubbed her shoulders some more, this time letting his hand slide beneath the collar of her silky blouse to the firm yet soft skin underneath. "Hey, it's not that I'm mean-spirited. I'll be rooting for their every fantasy to be fulfilled, I swear. It's just that I know how these things play out. I'm experienced, don't forget. I wanted a boy to play catch with. Look at me. I'm knee-deep in training bras and crushes on twelve-year-old gangly boys with voices that crack. The joke is on me, believe me.'' Jason shook his head ruefully and smiled, at least for the moment. While his hands were touching Catherine he was able to appreciate life's little jokes. Of course it helped that his darling daughter was a good two or three miles away.

"Ah, well," he said, skimming a finger along her neck, "I keep promising to get out of your hair, but I seem to be having problems getting out the door. Good night, Catherine.'' He studied her face for a moment, then tugged her closer, leaned down and kissed her. It was meant to be just a quick good-night salute, the bare minimum necessary for fulfilling the requirement after a date. But just the touch of her lips left Jason feeling needy. His libido recovered quite suddenly and quite nicely, and it was all he could do to stop himself from sweeping Catherine up into his arms and hauling her right up those steps behind her.

He should never have kissed her mouth. Her forehead maybe, or the tip of her nose—Jason was sure he could have kept either one of those fraternal. But that soft little rosebud mouth of hers—just look at it. Even now it was slightly pursed, begging for him to— Get a grip, Engel. Just get a grip. You have to go pick up your daughter. Remember her? Jason took a deep breath. "Good night, Catherine.'' The words came out sounding half-strangled, he had his teeth clenched so tightly.

"Good night, Jason," she whispered, oddly affected by that gentle little salute of a kiss.

"I'll bring over the ladder in the morning."

"All right," Catherine agreed, too fogged to argue.

Jason reached behind himself and opened the door a crack. "Oh, hell," he said and shut it again. He pulled Catherine into his arms and let loose the full power of his passion.

Catherine staggered under the onslaught of his marauding mouth. Good grief, the strength of a good pair of lips was not to be taken lightly. Man alive, Jason Engel was some kind of kisser. There was no way Catherine was going to push him away the way she should and walk away from this.

She put her hands on his shoulders. Not good enough. She slid them around his neck and hung on for dear life while she kissed him back.

Jason ran the tip of his tongue along the line where Catherine's lips met. She opened for him. When his tongue swept in, it was no subtle sneak attack, but rather a triumphant march, and Catherine was overwhelmed by the sensual onslaught. Jason slid a hand in between their bodies to cup her breast. Catherine knew she'd have collapsed in a puddle at his feet if it weren't for the strength of his supporting arm.

Catherine had never met a man capable of kissing with such passionate intent. She would have had her baby by now; heck, she would have had several of the little dears. Catherine had just enough presence of mind left to know she was a doomed woman if something didn't stop this soon. She thought about trying to pull herself back together. Thinking was about as far as it went, though.

Jason finally broke off the kiss himself. His chest ached. His head hurt from the blood pounding through his brain. He closed his eyes and reached for control. Damn, what was wrong with him?

Sex.

That was the extent of his horizon just then. Any haze disguising it during the day had burned away now. And what was the only constant in today's little equation?

Catherine.

Jason shook his head in silent denial.

No. *No, no, no, no, no.* He'd seen the way Catherine had lovingly handled the baby things she'd bought that morning, seen the way she'd dealt with Maura and Amy during the day. She'd even said so out loud; the woman wanted to be a mother. And she ought to have that opportunity. She'd be a natural. Sooner or later she'd start hearing a ticking in her head, if she hadn't already. And no way in hell would he even contemplate getting involved with another woman with a ticking biological clock. Absolutely not. From Jason's perspective, ticking biological clocks ranked right up there with timers on a stick of dynamite. They both had the same potential for blowing up, generally right in your face, too.

He looked down at her. Catherine was kind of swaying in place like she'd been through a windstorm and was still caught in the tail end. She looked mussed, her eyes were fogged over, and he thought she was adorable.

Hell, he could be in deep trouble here.

Jason took a deep breath and directed his arms to

let go. Several moments later they obeyed. "Sorry," he mumbled. "I got kind of carried away."

Catherine nodded absently while running her tongue over her lips. "Kind of," she said.

"I'll, um, see you."

Catherine was still nodding agreeably. "Right. See you, too."

Jason again reached for the knob behind him. "Ah, hell," he said. "One more for the road." He swept her back up against him, and they went through the whole thing all over again.

It was ten more minutes before Jason actually got himself out the door. Catherine had been no help, either. No help at all, he thought in a rather disgruntled fashion as he cut across the lawn between the two houses to get to his car.

Monica caught Catherine out in the parking lot after church services the following morning.

"So how'd the big day go yesterday?" Monica asked. "I couldn't believe it when Jason agreed to let me watch the girls so the two of you could go out to dinner together. This is so exciting. Your dream baby could well be on its way to reality and all with very little effort on our part, if you just don't blow this." Monica fluttered her lashes, clasped her hands over her breast and sighed meaningfully. "So give. Tell me everything."

Catherine stared at her sister. She'd been up late trying to sort out her feelings toward Jason Engel. She honestly had no idea of what they were, how she stood with him or anything else of cosmic significance in her own small universe. The man was dangerously attractive. The more she got to know him as a person, the more attracted she was. Was Monica right? Should she forget about trying to locate a sperm bank and go for the guy next door?

Finally she just shook her head and shrugged her shoulders at Monica. "I don't know what to say," she admitted.

Monica appeared ready to burst. "Well, say something," she implored. "I mean, come on, Catherine. There must be some little tidbit you can throw my way."

But for some unfathomable reason, Catherine, who up until this point in her life had been constitutionally unable to keep anything, anything at all from her sister didn't feel like sharing the details of last night. She didn't even want to talk about her day at the mall with Jason and the girls. It would be like divulging secrets, private things.

What had happened last night that was so special she couldn't talk about it, not even with her own sister?

Absolutely nothing. He'd picked her up; they'd gone to a terrific restaurant where they'd had great food and come home. Period. End of story.

Well, there was the way he had kissed her until she'd been oxygen deprived. At least, Catherine assumed that was why her vision had grayed out a couple of times during the thick of things. But, no, that was none of Monica's business. Catherine was turning over a new leaf. She was no longer the kind of date who kissed and told—not even her sister.

"Oh, look," Catherine said with relief. "Anna Freman is waving.'' Catherine waved back and smiled. ''She's coming over.''

Monica glanced over her shoulder. ''Darn,'' she said even as she smiled at the approaching Anna. ''We won't be able to talk at all once she gets going. Talk about your motor mouth.... *Anna,* how are you? It's been a month of Sundays since we've seen you. You look wonderful, so tanned.''

Anna beamed at the two sisters. ''You noticed. Thank you. I'm just back from Florida. I was helping my mother get settled into her new condo. Between sneaking out to sunbathe—it was in the seventies and low eighties the whole time I was there, if you can believe that, and helping Mom decorate, I had a blast. It's always so much more fun spending someone else's money, isn't it?''

''Oh, yes,'' Monica agreed. ''I've often said so myself. Listen, Anna, I'm glad everything's going so well with you and your mother, but Catherine and I need to talk—family business, you know. So, I'm sure you won't mind if we—I'll call you. We'll do lunch.'' Monica lost no time taking Catherine by the elbow and steering her away, leaving Anna gaping after them.

''That was certainly rude,'' Catherine said when Monica came to a halt two rows up and one over in the parking lot.

''Too bad. This is more important than what color she painted the walls in a condo hundreds of miles away that we'll never see. And yes, I see Robin Petowski over there, and if you wave at her, I'll kill you. Talk to me, Catherine.''

Catherine sighed. ''Look, Monica, I'll make a long

story very short. We went out to dinner. It was very nice, but no bells rang, no angels sang. He's a nice guy, but I don't think he's going to jump at any offers from me. I get the feeling he's been burned.''

Monica looked crestfallen. "Really?"

Catherine nodded. "Really."

"That's too bad."

"Yeah." Catherine shifted her feet and looked up at the sky. "Here comes that rain they were predicting. I just felt a drop hit my cheek. Temperature's dropping, too."

"I know, I know, you're getting cold and you want to go."

"Mon?" Don's deep male voice was decidedly impatient sounding as he called from their nearby car.

"You and Amy wait in the car, Don. Turn on the heater, warm it up. I'll be right there."

Catherine could hear her brother-in-law's sigh from two cars over.

"Fine," he said. "But I would like to get home so I can read the Sunday paper at some point this morning."

"I know, I know. Five minutes."

"No more, Monica," Catherine said. "I refuse to stand here any longer discussing last night. In case you haven't noticed, we're the only ones left. Everyone else has had the good sense to get in out of the rain."

"I can see there's not much point in talking to you any further."

"You got that right. I'm going home to paint my nursery. Once that's done I just know I'll have the courage to go see Dr. Perently."

Monica snorted. ''Yeah, right. I almost believe you.''

''Go away, Monica.'' And Catherine had to wonder why she was so concerned with checking for insanity in a donor's family. There was obviously enough in her own family that she ought not be so choosy.

Chapter Seven

Catherine changed into clothes appropriate for painting as soon as she got home. She went down the hall
to the room with the crib and stood in the doorway.
Cold November rain beat a slow staccato against the
window and filtered the light entering the room. Even
so, the window was large enough to compensate, and
on this gray, overcast day there was still enough light
entering through the paned glass to highlight the crib
leaning against the wall opposite the window.

The Crib.

The embodiment of everything she'd hoped and
dreamed for since she was a little girl playing with
baby dolls. She had been sidetracked briefly the year
Santa had brought her a wetting doll and her mother
had given birth to one of her brothers, what with
watching her mother change several messy diapers
and about twenty dolly diaper changes of her own,
but it had been only a momentary detour. Six months

later she'd decided she could handle even disgusting diapers so long as it was her own child's mess. Catherine had refused to help with Billy's, not even so much as to carry them to the diaper pail. And of course, her baby's diapers would not smell nearly as bad as Billy's, of that she'd been certain.

Catherine smiled to herself and entered the room. She reached the crib and ran her hand along one end. It was a beautiful white canopy crib. She'd taken it in at the shop four months ago and brought it home as third in a series. The first crib she'd fallen in love with, she'd never actually carted over to the apartment. It had been oak, stained golden and varnished until it gleamed. There'd been no decals, just some large-scale colored wooden beads threaded on metal spindles and set into the headboard. Catherine had kept it in the back room and mooned over that crib for nine months, the length of a pregnancy, she later realized. She'd loved that bed.

But then someone had brought in a walnut one with decals on the end of ducks wearing boots and carrying umbrellas. There'd been a crib skirt with matching padding to tie to the side rails and a coordinating soft sculpture wall hanging all still in perfect shape. Catherine had taken one good look and fallen in love all over again. That one, she'd brought home to the apartment, although she'd never actually gone so far as to set it up. The oak crib had eventually been put out on the store floor and sold six days later with only minor regrets.

I kept that walnut crib for almost two years, Catherine reminded herself as she rubbed her hand over the rail of this latest crib. But when this one came into the store, well, there was no comparison. It's perfect. Catherine sighed. This crib was going to get assembled, she swore. She went a step further every time. Once this one was put together and nestled over there in the corner, there'd be only one step left.

If only I could get on with the job of filling you up. You need a baby. It's what you were made for. Wistfully, she let her hand slide down one of the turned posts. And so was I. I'd be a good mother, darn it. It's not my fault I haven't met Mr. Right and gotten married yet. It's not. God knows I've tried to fall in love. It's difficult when the good ones all seem to be taken. She thought about her married friends. And frankly, a large percentage of the ones taken were only mediocre at best. Their wives were simply desperate women.

Catherine's head lifted at the sound of the doorbell.

She went down to answer it. A very damp Jason Engel stood on the other side. "Have you got a towel?" he asked by way of greeting. "I tried to run between the raindrops, but you lose your agility as you age, you know, and I got wet, anyway. I don't want to soak your floor."

"Jason!" Catherine said, still lost in her daydreams. "What are you doing here?"

Jason gave her a puzzled look and gestured to the left of her door. "I brought the stepladder. Remember? You said you needed one and I told you I'd bring mine over."

Catherine stuck her head out the door and sure enough, there was a nice, wooden five- or six-foot stepladder leaning up against the house.

"Where do you want it?"

"I didn't think you'd come out in the rain to do that, Jason. That's a little above and beyond the call of duty, but I do thank you. Come on in. I was just getting ready to start."

Jason picked up the ladder and carefully maneuvered it through the door opening. "You want this upstairs?"

"Yeah. That'd be good." Jason's hair was glistening with moisture making it appear almost black. She'd like nothing better than to get her hands into it, muss it up a little more. What would he say if she offered to dry it for him? Catherine wondered. Probably panic and take off like a fox being hunted. "I can take it from here if you've got things to do."

Jason kicked off his shoes, so he didn't track water, and started up the stairs. Catherine was wearing one of those oversize sweatshirts, just like the kind he always complained about Maura wearing. But on Catherine, it looked sexy as hell. It had at least half a dozen different colors of paint on it and a hole in one sleeve where she'd obviously caught it on something. The woman ought to be totally safe from a man's baser instincts in that kind of getup, but all Jason could think about was sliding his hands underneath there and rasping his thumbs over her nipples to make them peak.

The ladder wobbled as Jason staggered a bit at the idea of performing such a feat. Careful, old man, he cautioned himself. Catherine's not going to peak anything but her temper if you start taking out her light fixtures or putting holes in her walls.

"Where now?" he managed to say through lips

drawn thin from watching Catherine's hips sway up the steps in front of him.

"Oh, let's leave it in the hall." She indicated a spot next to the nursery. Fortunately she'd shut the door on her way downstairs. "I haven't laid out the drop cloths yet, so just put it here for now."

Jason took his eyes off her bottom with great difficulty and apologized, "I'm sorry, what did you say?" Concentrate, he admonished himself. Concentrate, damn it.

"Right here."

"Yes. Okay." He swung the ladder around and leaned it carefully against the wall. "Well, I need to get back. Maura and I had intended to rake the leaves and get them out onto the street for tomorrow's pickup, but our plans for the day went down the tubes when the rain started, so she decided to bake chocolate chip cookies. I need to get back and make sure she hasn't started any fires. If they're edible, she'll probably run some over. She said she was making them for you."

Catherine pushed her hair out of her face and stared at him. "You're kidding. Isn't that sweet?"

Jason checked to make sure the ladder was steady. "You haven't tasted her cookies yet."

"I'm sure they'll be fine."

"It's your stomach," he said, and started down the stairs. "Just shoo her back out the door when she stops over. Don't let her keep you from getting your stuff done. I'm going to try and do a little paperwork before the Bears game comes on at four. She can watch it with me. I'm still trying to train her to enjoy the sport, but she's not cooperating."

"I don't blame her. I don't like it very much, either."

Jason paused at the front door. "Baseball?"

"No. Too slow moving. They should reduce it to four innings. Then maybe I'd watch. No more than an hour, though."

Jason looked outraged. "Hockey?"

Catherine dismissed the entire sport with a flick of her hand. "Too violent. And none of them have any front teeth."

Jason rolled his eyes. "Do you like any sport at all?"

"I like figure skating. Oh, and ice dancing. They move so smoothly, don't they?"

Jason left.

Catherine laughed to herself as she started back up the stairs. She had brothers. She knew exactly what she'd been saying and the effect it would have on Jason. She'd gotten him out of the house before he'd thought to ask why she was doing an out-of-the-way bedroom before the first floor or her own room. She entered the room with the crib and picked up a tarp before snapping it open and settling it on the floor. The oak floor was entirely protected, and the paint cans opened and lined up when the doorbell rang again. Before Catherine could set down the roller she'd just picked up, she heard Maura's voice calling from the front vestibule.

"Catherine? Where are you? I opened the door and came in, is that okay?"

Catherine called downstairs. "Yes. Come on in, honey. I'm up here getting ready to paint."

Maura bounded up the stairs. "I baked cookies, and

I only had to throw out one batch! The others are fine now that I scraped some of the black off the bottoms. Dad said they were delicious and he was sure you'd like them, too, so I brought you a whole bunch.''

"Well how nice. Let's take them down to the kitchen, though, and have a glass of milk with them." Catherine figured they'd need something to wash the cookies down. Maura's description of her baking efforts did not inspire confidence. "I opened a can of paint, and it's already beginning to smell up here."

Maura reversed directions. She and Catherine wasted a good twenty minutes drinking milk and dunking cookies. They really weren't all bad. A little hard, but the milk went a long way toward alleviating that problem.

"So what are you painting?" Maura asked as she judged the remaining cookies carefully before selecting her fifth from the plate.

"Uh, just a bedroom, that's all."

Maura's eyes widened, and she perked up on her stool. "The one that's going to be the nursery?" she asked.

Man, she never should have opened her big mouth the other night. She should have just sat through that movie and suffered. Bringing out her quilting was going to come back and haunt her, Catherine just knew it. "Well, yeah, as a matter of fact it is. But that's our little secret, remember?"

Maura swallowed almost an entire cookie in her excitement. "I remember, I remember. Catherine, can I help? There's nothing to do at home, no homework or anything and I cleaned my room already, too. I'll be careful, I promise. Nobody's ever let me help paint before. Please?''

What could she do? What could she say? ''Uh, okay. I guess. You'll have to be very careful, though. Do exactly as I say.''

''I will,'' Maura breathed excitedly. ''Come on, let's go.'' And she took off, leaving her precious plate of cookies without another thought.

Over the course of the next hour, Maura and Catherine really got into the spirit of the thing. Maura rolled while Catherine edged. They opened the window a crack in an attempt to let out the paint fumes. But it was still raining pretty hard, so they couldn't open it much, just enough to dampen the sill and chill the room.

They had barely finished the first wall, singing along with the radio blasting from its position on the floor in the opposite corner when Jason burst into the room.

''Darn it, I've been ringing the bell and banging on the door for five minutes. What's going on? Why is the music so loud? Maura, you've been gone forever. How the heck long can it take to deliver a plate of cookies, for crying out loud? I thought we could play a game of Monopoly or Scrabble or something before the Bears game, spend some time together, but you never came back. What are you doing? You don't know how to paint. Catherine, you're insane. Maura, put that roller down and come home. This color is…interesting.''

Jason finally paused and took a breath. Catherine was relieved. She'd thought for a minute or so, toward the end, he was going to need rescue breathing. All right, so maybe she wasn't relieved. It might have been fun. "Maura's doing a fine job, Jason." And it was all going to get ragged over, anyway, but Maura didn't need to know that. "But if you two want to spend time together this afternoon, I guess I can spare her. Go ahead, honey. Trounce your dad for me."

Maura faced her father, roller in hand. "Dad, I don't want to play Scrabble or Monopoly. You always beat me."

Jason scratched his head and took a deep breath. "All right. What about Masterpiece?"

She waved the roller at him, her grip still strong. "You're always saying how much better it is to be a participant rather than a spectator. You made me try out for the volleyball team when I knew I didn't stand a chance of making it. Basketball, too. Look, I'm here. I'm doing. You should be happy. Come on, Dad, I really want to help Catherine."

Jason rubbed the back of his neck tiredly. His daughter was a master manipulator. Worse, every word she'd said was true. But they hadn't had much time together this week. He guessed that if he really wanted to do something with her, he was going to have to pick up a paintbrush and pitch in. "All right, all right. I'll stay and help, too. But just until the game."

"Jason, that's not necessary."

"Evidently it is if I want to see my daughter. Truthfully, I don't really mind. I'm getting tired of board games, too." He pushed up his sleeves and found the opened package of roller covers. He slipped one on a roller. "You've got enough supplies to equip a small army here," he said.

Catherine shrugged, not bothering to explain and went back to work. She'd only known him a few days, but she already knew better than to argue with him once his mind was set. "If you're sure."

"I'm sure," Jason grunted as he climbed the ladder and started rolling up by the ceiling. He didn't really bother glancing around until he'd climbed back down to redip the roller and move the ladder. The room was empty except for disassembled crib parts propped up on the unpainted wall across from him. He took a calming breath at the sight of it.

Don't panic, he instructed himself. It's got nothing to do with you.

"That the heirloom crib?" he asked. "The one that gets passed down to the youngest daughter?"

"What?" Catherine asked, momentarily confused. "Oh, right. That's it." What a stupid lie. All anybody had to do was take a good look at the thing to know it was too new to be an heirloom.

Jason nodded his head as he contemplated the crib and said, "Nice."

Catherine's eyes moved back and forth between Jason and the crib, trying to see what he was seeing, trying to gauge his reaction. "I like it," she said.

"It's in pretty good shape for something that must have been through a whole slew of babies."

"Uh, yeah. Everyone's been very careful, I guess."

Jason set his roller down. Cautiously, as though it might blow up in his face at any moment, he approached the crib. He touched it tentatively then ran his hand along the side rail. "We had a white crib for Maura," he said. "But it had an elephant wearing a pink tutu and pink slippers dancing like a ballerina up on her toes. I remember there were sheets that matched. And there was a bassinet thing for when she was really little. Wicker with a mattress in it no bigger than a grown person's regular pillow."

"Cute," Catherine said, watching Jason curiously.

"Yeah, it was. I remember when we brought her home from the hospital and put her into that crib for the first time. I made Karen do it. I was afraid I'd drop her or something. Maura was so little, she looked lost in that great big bed."

"Did I really, Daddy?"

"Yeah, you did. That was when I went and bought the bassinet."

Catherine was getting all misty eyed just listening to Jason's reminiscences.

"Maura's skin had this pink cast to it then."

"It still does."

"Yeah. It was even more noticeable as a baby, though. Newborns are really red. You wouldn't believe it. Until somebody told me it would fade, I was a little worried for a while there. By the time we brought her home, she was just pink." Jason grasped a turned end post and looked off into the distance. "And she was all wrapped up like a mummy in this pink receiving blanket." Jason grinned lopsidedly at his daughter who listened in rapt attention. "I thought she had to be the most beautiful baby in the world. Just looking at Maura scared me to death back then, still does, but she was so sweet looking. So unbelievably sweet."

Catherine walked over to the crib and put her hand over Jason's. "I'll bet."

"My mother took to calling her 'Pinkie Sweetie,'

as a matter of fact. Stupid nickname stuck for years. It was a real effort to remember to call her Maura when she started nursery school. That doll Maura got the baby things for even though she's put away now? Her name is Pinkie Sweetie. Maura named her after herself.''

Maura was, in fact, turning pink as her father let all her secrets out of the bag, but it didn't faze Jason. He kissed her on her paint spattered forehead. ''That'll teach you to leave and not come back. Next time I'll think of something even more embarrassing. Remember that.'' He had to give himself a shake to chase the memories away. He met Catherine's eyes, looking faintly red himself. ''Enough of that. You probably think I'm some kind of idiot by now.''

''No.'' She denied the possibility.

''Yeah, well, you wouldn't be far wrong.'' He rubbed his hands briefly together and glanced around the room. ''All right. What do you want me to do next? Here or over there?''

''Maura, run down and bring up the cookies, all right? I'm having a chocolate attack.''

''Actually, there's a box of fudge cookies at home sitting on the counter. Why don't you get those, too? For variety, you know.''

''Oh, okay. I think we already ate most of the other ones, anyway.''

''Thanks, sweetie.'' Catherine waited until she'd left the room, then turned back to Jason. ''You start right here,'' she said, and reached up to tug his head down to hers. ''You are the sweetest man. Whether you want to be or not, you are. No wonder your mom called her Pinkie Sweetie. She was seeing a little bit of you in her.'' Catherine kissed him.

Jason's heart stuttered, but he wasn't about to let a little thing like a heart attack keep him from wrapping his arms around Catherine, not if she was wanting it enough to initiate things herself.

"No man worthy of the name wants to be called sweet," he muttered, then crushed her to him, unwilling to waste any more energy over the insult.

Sweet. Hah! He'd give her sweet. Jason deepened the kiss she'd initiated, taking control away from her. Catherine melted against him, and Jason staggered a step or two as her body fused itself to hers.

He slipped his hands up underneath her baggy sweatshirt and let them roam over her bare back. Her skin was smooth, like satin. When he followed the line of the back of her bra with his finger, she sighed into his mouth. Jason found himself nearly supporting her. Undoubtedly, this was not the time or the place, but he couldn't help himself. He unhooked it.

Catherine gasped and broke the kiss. She tipped her head back and looked up into his face, her eyes wide. Silently they studied each other. Slowly Jason let one hand drift. It traveled along her waist, migrating from her back to her side and on to her midriff. Then it headed due north. All the while Jason watched her carefully for any sign of refusal.

What he saw was a bit of confusion.

More of anticipation.

Then, when he found his goal and her breast rested plumply in his hand, there was wonder, pure and simple.

Her eyes blinked shut, and the small, blissful smile

she wore told Jason more clearly than words that Catherine was a sensual woman fully engaged in savoring the sensations he, Jason Engel, was bringing to life in her.

Well, he could get serious, too.

Jason slowly lowered his mouth back onto hers while he gently brushed her nipple. It was velvet soft in his palm, and he worried that his hand might be too rough, but Catherine wore such a look of bliss, he doubted it was much of a problem.

He edged her sweatshirt up, got ready to move his mouth on down the line. His whole body was tense and aching with anticipation. He wanted to taste her—now. But he didn't want to spoil things by frightening her. He forced himself to slow down. To savor her, to—

"Okay, guys, I've got the cookies," Maura called from downstairs. "Should I bring up the milk and some cups, too? Or do you want to come down here?"

Jason's head popped up and Catherine's eyes opened. They stared at each, dazed.

"Daddy? Catherine? You're still up there, aren't you?"

"We're here, pumpkin." After several deep breaths and a lot of silent swearing, Jason was finally able to answer his daughter's calls. "Right here." He pulled Catherine to him for a brief hug full of regret, then reached behind her and rehooked her bra. "I'm sorry," he whispered into her hair. "So sorry."

For what? Catherine wondered hazily, feeling as though she'd just ridden a hurricane. She held her head with her hands to stop its spinning.

"Come on, you guys, answer me," Maura yelled. "What do you want me to do?"

Jason cleared his throat and set Catherine away from him. She wobbled and he steadied her before removing his arm. Jason winced when he saw that Catherine was now using the crib to support herself. The crib, for crying out loud. Talk about your basic in-your-face consequence reminders.

"We're coming down," he yelled. "Be right there." Jason glanced around the room, suddenly wondering why Catherine had picked this out-of-the-way room to decorate. The crib was the only piece of furniture in it. He took Catherine's arm and guided her out the doorway. "Let's go," he said. "Before she comes up here to get us."

Catherine let Jason support her down the stairs, but stopped by the half bath off the front hall to wash her hands and rinse her flushed cheeks. Jason used the bath when she was done. Catherine went on to the kitchen. Maura had found the under-the-counter radio, turned it on and was humming along while she arranged cookies on a plate. She was using the kitchen table, her back to the rest of the room.

Catherine took the milk out of the refrigerator, set it on the counter and closed the refrigerator. Then she leaned back against the cool metal door she'd just shut. "Holy cow," she muttered reverently, after assuring herself Maura wouldn't be able to hear over the sound of the radio.

"I think Jason just had an unbelievably narrow escape for a man with his view of parenthood. I do believe I just came mighty close to having my fondest dream fulfilled."

Catherine closed her eyes momentarily. "The weird thing is, I'm only just now realizing it. I wasn't thinking about anything up there at all except for what he was doing to me. My mind was gone, totally gone. God, that man is potent. I really, seriously, am beginning to believe that Monica might have a point. The question is, what the heck do I do about it? How do I approach Jason with a request like this? I'd only die a thousand deaths if he turned me down. Of course I'd die a thousands deaths if he said yes, too."

Somehow Catherine pulled herself together enough to get three tumblers of milk and a handful of napkins over to the table.

The three of them sat around the table and had a totally normal conversation. They demolished the cookies, drank all her milk and discussed how the rain made Maura's hair frizz. Catherine accidentally clinked her cup on her front teeth, Maura teased Jason for having a crumb on his chin, and the room smelled faintly of the upstairs fresh paint—totally normal.

Catherine took it all in and tried to figure out how she felt about it. She had just had what amounted in her book to practically a conversion experience upstairs, and they were all acting like nothing had happened. It was too bizarre for words.

Pushing herself up from the table, she said, "Well, let's get back to it." Like Scarlett O'Hara, she'd decided to think about it tomorrow. She didn't know what else to do.

They couldn't hear the rain over the music they blasted, and proceeded to spend the entire afternoon cocooned in the small room, painting and singing along. Jason had a terrific baritone. And, he forgot about the Bears game. Catherine took note of that. She rather thought it might be significant.

Rain continued to fall outside and the temperature continued to drop. Even though they began to squint as more of the walls were covered with the garish golden yellow undercoat, their spirits were not dampened. The threesome found they worked well together, and more, they enjoyed each other's company. It was a surprising revelation. In point of fact, there was a low-key but undeniable party going on in that room. They ended the day by ordering pizza.

"It was fun," Catherine later told her sister. "We ate an entire extralarge pepperoni pizza and swilled enough root beer to float a battleship. I was sick all night, but we really had a good time together."

"We're getting old," Monica said with a sigh. "I can't eat pepperoni pizza anymore, either, without feeling sick. Of course, you'd better get used to heartburn. What you felt last night is nothing compared to what you'll feel when you're pregnant. Anything the slightest bit greasy and you practically have to go to bed for a week to recover. And everybody's always shoving glasses of milk in your face. Yuck."

"I like milk," Catherine told her sister. "We had a lot of that, too. What is all that banging in the background? What are you doing?"

"I was in the kitchen when you called, so I'm putting the clean dishes away. If we talk long enough I may even get the mountain of dirty ones in the sink washed and into the drainboard. Now, what about Jason. Did he kiss you? Give you any indication at all that he's starting to think along more personal lines?"

Catherine wasn't about to discuss Jason's kissing her with her sister. It had been too personal. That was, of course, how she knew she was in trouble. How could anything be too personal to share with your very own sister? Your brothers, sure, anyone could understand reticence there. They'd have ragged her for a month of Sundays. But her sister?

Instead, she talked about The Baby Plan. Somehow it seemed far less personal than Jason's kisses. "I'm just not sure of anything anymore, Monica," she began carefully. "I was so positive the sperm bank was the right way to go, but last night I realized you might be right. You should have heard Jason talk about Maura as a baby. I practically cried, it was so sweet. On the other hand, the man gets positively hyper when he runs into any of the baby things I'm getting ready for the shop. I don't know if he'd willingly agree to giving me a baby or spit in my eye."

Monica sighed gustily into Catherine's ear. "You'd really be going out on a limb. What a bite in the butt."

"Yeah."

"Darn it, Catherine, you're just going to have to take the chance. This would be too perfect. So much less wear and tear on your emotions. No running back and forth to some impersonal clinic and their anonymous vials of—"

"Don't start, Monica," Catherine felt compelled to warn.

"And what if it didn't work the first time? It probably wouldn't. It took us six months of trying for Amy. And that was with several shots at it per month, for crying out loud."

Catherine did not want to hear this. The tips of her ears were reddening as she listened to her sister rant. "Monica!" she wailed.

But Monica was not to be deterred. "Here is this perfect guy—good looks, handsome as sin, sincere as all get-out—living only a few feet away. How much more convenient can it get? If it doesn't take the first time, hey no problem. You ask him to meet you halfway, and the two of you roll out your back doors and give it another try."

Catherine's brow furled at that. She was in her kitchen, and she studied her back door dubiously. "You expect us to do this in the backyard?"

"If you're going to be so literal, you can wait till it's dark and put up a hammock."

"It's November. It's cold now and only going to get colder. Maybe I should wait for spring before I approach him," Catherine suggested hopefully.

"You're missing the point," Monica told her. "Now, did he kiss you? Tell me he did. How would you rate it? On a scale of one to ten."

"That's none of your business." Catherine cleared her throat. "Ten. Twelve. I don't know. Good. Very good."

Monica pounced. "Ah-hah!"

"Monica, I'm not going to say there haven't been certain...indications..."

"Yes? Yes?"

Catherine walked over to the back door and looked out its window. Visually, she measured the distance between Jason's back entrance and her own. There. Right there. That point on the lot line would be just about halfway. "I mean, certainly it's *possible*, actually more than possible that Jason might feel some sort of sexual attraction to me.''

''Ohh. That's good. That's very good.''

Catherine squinted, trying to visualize Jason and her—together—there on the lot line. It was the low point for both their yards and underwater from yesterday's rain. It was difficult to picture the scene. She cleared her throat. ''Monica, would it be very, very bad of me if, well, what if Jason was to, um, lose his head at some point when we were together, kissing, you know. And say I was to more or less keep my mouth shut about my lack of birth control until after things were, uh, irreversible so to speak—''

''The deed would be done and he none the wiser until it was too late?''

''Yeah.''

''It's an idea. Hmm. Play on man's basic fixation with sex and just simply don't tell him that while he's using you, you're using him. It has potential, Cath.''

Catherine turned away from the back door and its view of the yard. She faced her sink, in which sat a plate of semiburned chocolate chip cookies and three cups with dried milk rings in the bottom. She knew which one had been Jason's without even having to think about it. It was her turn to sigh. ''It's a lousy idea. Monica, I've finally found a guy whose genetic code actually comes in second to everything else I like about him, I mean the attraction is just *incredible*—everything you used to say about Don, only I could never understand it. But everything's wrecked because I like the guy too much to trick him like that. He matters to me, Monica. He matters a lot.''

''You are in a mess, aren't you?''

"Looks that way from where I'm sitting," Catherine agreed miserably.

"You don't think he'd forgive you, once he had a chance to cool down?"

"He might never even realize he'd been tricked. I could just act like whatever I tell him I'd been using must have failed. That's not the point. I'd know. He's a good man, really trying hard to be a good father to his daughter. He's just feeling a little overwhelmed and inadequate right now. The thing is, unfortunately, I don't think I could live with using him like that."

"He really *has* gotten to you."

"I know." And the knowledge was making her miserable.

"Well, I don't know what to tell you, sweetie. This is getting a whole lot more complicated than I ever anticipated."

"Tell me about it."

"I'm out of pans to wash. As far as I can see, all you can do is ask. The worst he can do is say no. If I come up with anything more brilliant, I'll give you a call."

"All right. Goodbye, Monica."

"Bye, Cath. Buck up."

"Yeah, right."

Chapter Eight

Catherine spent all her free time the following week, finishing up the nursery. Maura showed up several times in the early evening to help for an hour or two. The two of them cut up an old T-shirt of hers and dunked their rags into a lighter shade of yellow paint. They wrung them out and dropped them into their palm, letting them form a loose wad which was then rolled up and down the walls. It left a delicate lacelike pattern behind that overlaid the deep gold first coat. The second layer of ragging overlaid all of that with the palest yellow she'd bought and when the two of them stepped back to look at the first finished wall, Catherine knew the paint saleswoman had been right. This nursery was going to be spectacular, one any baby would be proud to sleep in.

She really resented Jason Engel that whole week, too. Partially it was because he already had his baby and she didn't. But also, he'd spoiled her project for her. His help that first day had really brought home to Catherine what she'd be missing all her subsequent days—what she'd been missing all her adult life. A partner. Someone to love. Someone to share her chores—and her passions with. That darn spontaneous painting cum pizza party hadn't left Catherine with much to look forward to—unless she talked him into her plan. And even then it would be no better than half a loaf. She was suddenly afraid that now she wanted the whole thing.

She worked hard at the store on Saturday, rearranging the newborn section. Another crib came in, but after a brief study of it, Catherine decided she liked the canopy one at home better. That was good, because the bunny on this one was wearing blue, and she'd hate to have to repaint her yellow walls after all the effort she'd put in.

Elephants, bunnies, bears, what did it matter? There was no little Pinkie Sweetie to put under their care. When she got home, Catherine put a TV dinner in the oven and went upstairs to stand in the doorway to the nursery. It was beautiful. Everything she'd ever pictured in her mind. Sill-length white sheer tiebacks now filtered the light from the setting sun. The room glowed as the pinkened rays brought the walls alive. She'd also finally set up the crib. The wall she'd chosen to display it against made the little bed the focal point of the room. The effect was an absolute knockout. There was no other word to describe it. Too bad there was no baby to take advantage of the room she'd so lovingly created.

She sighed, turned her back on the room and went

downstairs to eat her TV dinner. Alone.

As always.

Maura came in through the back door around seven-thirty that night after a perfunctory knock. She had Jason in tow. "Hi, Catherine," she said. "I want my dad to see the room we painted. I figured he'd already seen the crib so we don't need to worry about not telling secrets to him."

Jason had been relaxed looking when he'd come in; now his head swung sharply around. His gaze impaled Catherine while he questioned his daughter. "What's that supposed to mean? What secret?"

"Daddy, you mean you didn't figure it out? Man, are you dense or what?"

Catherine grimaced. "Maura, you shouldn't speak to your father like that."

"Yeah, Maura," Jason seconded, stupidly pleased to have Catherine stand up for him. "You shouldn't speak to me like that."

Maura rolled her eyes. "Come look. You'll see."

Catherine tried to think, but her brain must have blown a few synapses and her neuron connectors weren't connecting—or something. At any rate, nothing came to her. "Uh, Maura—"

"He's got to see, Catherine," Maura whined. "We worked so hard on it, and it's so totally awesome now."

Catherine sighed. What the heck. Maybe this would bring things to a head. She gestured toward the hall and stairwell. "Go ahead." But she waited in the kitchen. She filled the coffeemaker. The smell of the freshly ground beans quickly scented the air. Nervously she sat at the table listening to the sound of footsteps overhead and unintelligible voices echoing. A few minutes later she heard them coming down the stairs, in the front hall, entering the kitchen. "So," she said, glancing over her shoulder. "What'd you think? Maura and I do good work together, huh?"

Jason stared at her steadily. "Very. Maura, you haven't practiced your flute yet today, and it's getting late. You run along home and get started. I'll follow in just a little while. I want to talk to Catherine for a minute."

"But, Daddy—"

"Later, pumpkin, not now. You've had lots of alone time with Catherine so far this week, and I haven't had any. It's my turn. Don't forget your scales."

Once Maura was out of the way, Jason moved over to the coffeemaker. "Do you mind if I pour myself a cup? I need the jolt. You must want some as well. I'll do the honors," he said as he opened the upper cabinet and took out two mugs.

Catherine nodded. "Thanks."

Jason filled them both, then came over to the table. He sat down and pushed one of the mugs in front of her. "About that heirloom crib—I got a closer look at it just now."

Catherine ran a hand through her hair and sighed. "It's not an heirloom. I brought it home from the shop."

Jason nodded. "That's sort of what I thought. One usually doesn't associate plastic with antiques. The vinyl teething strip on the railing was sort of a dead giveaway."

"You're very observant." Restlessly she drummed

her fingers against the mug. Should she ask him? What if he said no? What if he said yes?

Jason sat back and observed her carefully over the top of his mug. "Catherine, are you pregnant with somebody's baby?"

She blinked. "What? For heaven's sake. No. Of course not."

Steam curled in front of his face, partially obscuring her view. "Then what's with the crib? That's a lot of work to go through for nothing. I know you mentioned wanting to become a mother. Maybe you're planning on adopting?"

Catherine twirled a finger in her hair. "Not exactly." She took a deep breath. "Funny you should bring this up, Jason, because I've been meaning to ask you something."

He eyed her levelly. "What?"

She sipped her coffee; she studied the inside of the mug as though it held the secret of life; she stared at the ceiling in much the same fashion. "Jason, I want a baby of my own. Adoption lists are from here to eternity, and a single person is at the eternity end. Besides, I want to experience pregnancy and birth. I read that infant-mother bonding was more easily achieved that way, too. I'm selfish. I admit it. I want the whole package." Catherine chanced a look at him to see how he was receiving all this, but his expression was frustratingly unrevealing.

"I adore Maura. I would kill to have a child just like her. Jason, would you ever consider giving me a baby?"

Jason jerked back in his seat as though she'd shot him. Catherine knew she'd shocked him. Men were so damnably unperceptive. Why couldn't he have put two and two together for himself, done the gentlemanly thing and offered before she'd had to ask? She felt herself turning red.

"Catherine, I don't think—"

"I would take full responsibility. Once I was pregnant you'd be totally off the hook. You wouldn't have to support the baby, spend time with it, nothing. I would handle it all."

"If that's supposed to make me more receptive to this crazy idea, you've missed the boat," Jason growled. He got up and began to prowl the kitchen. "You ask too much, Catherine. What am I, made of stone, that you think I could knowingly make a baby with you, then walk away? Have a child of mine one door down and not acknowledge it in any way? Did you think about my needs at all when you came up with this little plan? I don't believe this." He dumped his mug into the sink and watched the coffee stain spread. Turning on the faucet, he rinsed it all down, staring at it long after it had vanished. "With everything I've gone through with Maura you could ask this of me?"

Catherine shrank in her chair. "I was thinking of what you'd been through with Maura," she whispered. "That's why I wanted to assure you I'd be totally responsible."

"To purposefully bring a baby into this world assumes a willingness to take on the responsibility for that new life on the part of *both* parents, as far as I'm concerned. That's why my heart bleeds for Maura. She's only got one parent willing to come through for her. I could never— No. Just—no." And he left.

Catherine sat at the kitchen table for a long time before finally rising, flipping the bolt on the back door and going to her room. She stared at the ceiling until the darkness began to gray. Birds were beginning to call outside the window when she finally drifted to sleep.

She dragged herself out of bed a few hours later. It was Sunday. Monica would be expecting her at church. When she got there, Monica invited her for Sunday dinner, which she declined.

Catherine decided then and there that this particular funk was worth wallowing in. She deserved it. She got in her car and sat in the church parking lot, unable to turn the key. Unfortunately, Catherine was also a natural optimist and go-getter. She had no idea how to really get into the spirit of this depression. Heck, what was she supposed to do? She was in the middle of a personal crisis, for crying out loud, maybe not midlife, but close enough. Tapping the steering wheel, Catherine thought. She'd gone out and gotten everything she'd set out to get all leading to this one goal. Her life had been carefully planned so that when the time came, she'd be in a position to juggle both a career and family life. She had the career, the house, even the damn nursery, so where was the family?

Catherine sat there and continued to tap the steering wheel for long moments.

"Oh, the hell with this." Enough was enough.

She turned on the ignition and headed out onto the street. "Where did I see that place?" she asked herself as she drove along. "Was it on McKinley? No, Jefferson. Could it have been Bittersweet? How far down?"

Eventually she found the garden center. It was so late in the season, all their spring bulbs were on clearance. "I'll take whatever you've got left of those red tulips," she told the man behind the counter. "They'll match my front door."

He scratched his head and looked at her through thick lenses. "That'd be maybe three, three and a half dozen."

"Is that enough? I want the house to look cheerful come spring."

"Got anything there now?"

Catherine shifted her feet. "I don't know. I don't think so."

"You need about ten, twelve dozen to really look good when they come up," he informed her.

She blinked. "That many?"

He nodded. "Yep."

She blew out a puff of air, walked over to the picked-over bins of bulbs and began pointing. "Well, then, I guess I'll take these and the rest of those. And we might as well throw in some of the daffodils over there. Will that be enough to look good?"

The man grunted and nodded. "That'll do you." He came out from behind the counter with some brown paper sacks and began bagging bulbs for her. He took a pencil from the center-front pocket of his overalls and marked on the bags the numbers of bulbs and variety names as well as planting instructions for her.

"Best get them in the ground right away," she was informed as he took her money. "Gettin' kind of late."

Catherine was a little dismayed when she saw the

size of the pile of spring bulbs she'd purchased in an attempt to cheer herself up. What had she just done? She hoped she had them planted by Christmas. You could forget Thanksgiving. That was only a week and a half away. Catherine had a mental image of herself out in front with a pickax, chopping away at the frozen earth in the middle of January.

This was all Jason Engel's fault.

Bitter all over again, she drove the rest of the way home.

Maura and Jason were outside raking when she got there. Catherine waved, one brief up-and-down motion of her hand, then went inside to change out of her church things. She bundled herself up in warm clothes; the temperature had dropped considerably over the course of the week. That was to be expected during November, of course, but it didn't help her any in facing the prospect of getting twelve dozen spring bulbs into the ground.

The sky was gray, she noticed when she went back out. Not unusual for November, but it did nothing to improve her mood. Catherine just hoped the snow or rain or whatever held off long enough for her to rake the lawn and get at least a portion of the small mountain of bulbs she'd purchased into the ground.

This was stupid. Really, really stupid. Feeling disgruntled and more than a little put-upon, Catherine trudged out into the yard. Darn Jason Engel's rotten hide, anyway. She didn't need him or his baby. She didn't need anything from anybody. She would busy herself tending her store and her bulbs and she would be happy, damn it. Happy.

"Hi, Catherine," Maura sang from next door.

Catherine was marching from the garage to the front of her house, rake shouldered like a rifle. She wished it was. She'd like to shoot Maura's father. He was nothing more than a—a selfish sperm hoarder, that's what he was. However, Maura had nothing to do with that. She relented. "Hi, honey," she called back.

"Dad and I are almost finished with our leaves. Want us to come help you when we're done?"

Catherine was already cold, but frostbite was preferable than facing Jason again. "No, that's all right," she called back. "You and your dad have done your part," she said. "You two go on in and warm up when you're done. I'll be fine." She always had been; she was now; and she always would be.

She raked for about ten minutes before Jason and Maura crossed the property line, rakes still in hand. They said nothing, just dug right in. Jason moved twice the volume of leaves with each sweep of his rake as either Catherine or Maura. Catherine hated him for that alone and virtually accosted him. "What are you doing?" she asked.

Jason leaned on his rake. "Helping out. Being neighborly."

"I don't need any help. I'm doing just fine all by myself."

Jason reached out to tuck a strand of blowing hair back behind her ear. "I'm sure you're a big girl and capable of doing this all on your own, but I feel like helping you, all right?"

He looked away, then back to her. He made an impatient sound. "Look, Catherine, I'm sorry about last night. I know I disappointed you, and I guess I ought to be flattered you thought enough of me to ask. I didn't mean to be impatient, you just caught me by surprise, that's all. My answer would have been the same, I just wish I'd handled things better, but what's done is done. Now just be quiet and let me do this for you, okay? Here's a project I can at least help you out with.''

It was obvious he wasn't going to leave. Heck, he was already out there swinging that rake like he'd just stepped out the door, fresh and raring to go. Reluctantly Catherine joined in, but it wasn't long before she realized that simply being in the same yard with Jason was a constant and painful reminder of the collapse of all her dreams. Well, the sooner she got rid of him, the sooner she could start getting over all of this. Catherine raked like all the demons of hell were after her. They finished the entire lawn in forty-five minutes.

''There,'' she said, a bit breathlessly. ''It's done. Thanks a lot. I appreciate it. Bye.''

Jason nodded. He sighed. Catherine obviously wasn't about to forgive him for his refusal of last night. He felt badly for her, it was obvious to him she'd make a good mother, but honestly, what had she expected? ''You're welcome,'' he said.

He stared after her as she swung her hips on her way to put her rake back in the garage. Jason wanted the soft woman who'd melted in his arms and kissed him like she was sipping the secret of life itself from his lips when their mouths met. He lusted after that woman. This one was as prickly as a—a—something with spines, that was what. Damn, he didn't need this. None of this was his fault. Catherine was the crazy one, not him. "Come on, Maura. Let's go put a pizza in and heat up some apple cider."

"Okay, Dad." Maura looked back and forth between her father and the driveway Catherine had disappeared down in a puzzled fashion before turning to follow. "I'm coming."

Catherine carried the rake back to her garage, muttering all the way. "Stupid man," she said, and propped the rake up against the front wall of the garage. Grabbing a spade, Catherine stalked around to the rear of her car and popped the trunk.

Looping the handles of the large plastic bag holding all the smaller bags of bulbs over one wrist, Catherine tucked a small cube of peat moss under her arm. She slammed the trunk down and, dragging the spade behind, made her way back to the front of the house. "Men," she muttered as she dropped everything in a pile on her front sidewalk. "They're such jerks. No wonder I haven't met Mr. Right yet. He's a figment of the feminine imagination. He doesn't exist in the real world."

Catherine held on to her anger and nurtured it. Without it, she had nothing. Nothing at all. Well, there was the cold, and she was rapidly becoming frozen through. Every stab of her spade into the black soil fed her frustration. "Take that," she said, picturing Jason's head and transferred another shovelful of dirt to the sheet she'd set next to the hole she was digging. Catherine sent the spade back for another bite of the soil. "And that." A shiver took her. "Holy Moses, it's cold out here." She took her gloves off to blow on her fingers.

It didn't get much more miserable than this, Catherine decided. Her one and only dream in life shattered and every extremity on her body willing to follow suit. She had hours to go before she got the only babies she'd probably ever have, to sleep in their beds for the winter. Catherine pulled her glove back on with her teeth and took aim with the blade of her shovel one more time.

"What are you doing now?" a deep male voice boomed behind her.

"Umph." Catherine jumped and lost her grip on the shovel handle. It dropped right on her foot. "Ouch! Damn it! I would have sworn they were too cold to feel anything, but that hurt." She twisted around to see Jason standing on her lawn. The man seemed determined to cause her pain in one way or another. "Go away," she said, and ungraciously turned her back on him. She reached down for the spade handle. "I've got work to do."

And with a temper like that, Jason thought, he just might leave her there to do it all by herself. He half turned away, determined to leave, then sighed, knowing he couldn't. He pivoted back. Poor woman, thought Jason. It had been unintentional, and his answer would have to be the same today, but he'd hurt her the night before. She looked so miserable now. Her nose was red, her cheeks were windburned and she was all huddled up in a vain attempt to protect herself from the wind. No wonder she was snappish. She appeared brittle enough to break.

"Catherine, you want to tell me why you're standing out in the wind digging up your garden?" He questioned her in what he hoped was a reasonable tone of voice, but it was an effort. To be out here in weather like this showed she didn't have even as much brainpower as God instilled in little gray geese. Why, Catherine Nicholson quite literally hadn't enough sense to come in out of the cold.

"I needed some cheering up," Catherine grudgingly admitted, when it became obvious Jason intended to stand there until she answered him.

"So you thought you'd go outside and play in the freezing cold? This is going to make you feel better?"

"So I thought putting tulips in might do the trick," Catherine spat out. "But it's hard because I bought a lot of bulbs and the ground is like concrete. Now I'd appreciate it if you'd get out of my way, I have a lot of work to do."

"Catherine, tulips aren't going to cheer you up until next spring. All it's going to do right now is hurt your back."

"I know that," she snapped. Did she ever. She'd be lucky if she ever straightened out her spine again. "It was all I could think of at the time, all right?"

Jason held his hands up in self-defense. "Hey, I'm just trying to understand what's going on, that's all. I told you I have trouble with the female mind. You knew that."

No more than she had with the male mind. Catherine took a used tissue out of her coat pocket and blew her nose. "Jason, its supposed to get cooler as the week goes on. We might even get snow. I have a million bulbs to plant before that happens. As a special favor to me for everything I've done for your daughter, go away. Please."

Jason looked at the stack of bags waiting on her sidewalk. She really did have a million bulbs lying there. "Why'd you buy so many?" he asked, astonished. "You've got enough there to landscape the entire block and then some."

"Because I felt the need of *serious* cheering up, okay?" Catherine was beginning to feel foolish.

Personally, Jason thought whoever had sold Catherine all those bulbs had taken advantage of her gullibility. He was no doubt on his way south for the winter after dumping the last of his fall wares on Catherine.

Jason sighed. He ought to just ignore this whole mess. It was Catherine's problem. He had enough troubles of his own without borrowing more. But there was something about Catherine that made it impossible for him to ignore her misery, even if it was self-inflicted. He knew he was responsible for her bad mood. Oh, yes, he knew.

Jason took the shovel away from her. "Go in and get some hot cider from Maura," he directed. "There's still some on the rangetop. There may even be a slice of pizza left if my waiflike, delicate, darling daughter didn't snarf it down. Don't come back out until you've warmed up. By then I'll have this dug up for you."

"I don't want you to—"

"Too bad. It'll take me half as long as it would take you. I'm bigger than you, and I intend to win, so move."

"Jason—"

"Now."

It was futile. Catherine gave in. "He sure is pushy," she grumbled as she rounded the back of his house. "He sure likes to stick his nose in and take over. Hey, Maura, what's up?'' she asked as she entered Jason's home.

"The sky."

Now, Maura she understood. Maura was on her wavelength. "Got anything hot left?"

"What's Dad doing?" Maura asked as she handed Catherine a steaming mug.

"Digging up my front yard for me so I can put some tulip bulbs in before it snows."

"Weird."

"I just wanted a little cheering up," Catherine muttered, and winced as she burned her tongue. "I wasn't thinking what a project it would turn into."

"I meant that he would go out and do that."

"Oh."

"He hates gardening and stuff. The only reason we went out and raked was because the last leaf pickup is tomorrow."

"You mean he doesn't make a habit of taking over other people's gardening tasks?"

Maura giggled at that. "Absolutely not. It's so strange, because he hates painting, too. I found this totally awesome blue color I've been trying to get him to paint my bedroom for the longest time. I bugged him so much he bought the paint when we were at the home center one day. That was months and months ago. He's always got some excuse or another why he can't do it, but he helped you right off the bat. You didn't even have to nag."

Catherine was insulted at that. "I don't nag. Your father is simply pushy."

"He never has been before."

"How bizarre."

"Yeah."

Catherine finished her cider. There had been no pizza left. Jason knew his daughter, Catherine guessed, so she drew her gloves on and went back out.

Jason stuck with her while they mixed peat moss and bone meal into the dirt and buried all one hundred and forty-four bulbs. They filled the front evergreen beds and hid them in large circular areas they created around two trees. Tulip and daffodil bulbs would march down both sides of the sidewalk and would overwhelm the mailbox post come April and May.

If Catherine so much as frowned, once those blossoms popped, Jason told himself when he finally began to defrost over another steaming mug of cider two hours later, he would damn well feed her tulip bulbs for breakfast, lunch and dinner every day for the rest of her life.

The mug stopped halfway to his mouth. The rest of her life? Where had that come from? He wouldn't be around long enough to carry out any such threat, would he?

No, certainly not. Surely she would grow tired of playing house and move away after a few years. Hell, *he'd* move away, if need be.

It would be worth it to save his sanity.

But Maura liked this neighborhood. She was finally forming friendships after a rough year and a half of adjustments. No, Catherine would have to be the one to move away. But he didn't want her to move. He wanted everything to go back to the way it was before she'd hit him with her bomb the night before. Damn, why'd she have to go and spoil things? He'd been enjoying her company, fantasizing about her fancy underwear, having good times together with and without Maura. Why couldn't that have been enough?

"Dad?"

"Hmm?"

"I thought you hated outdoor stuff. You carried on enough about having to rake the leaves. You said that was why you went to college—so you could make enough to pay somebody else to do the jobs you didn't like. Remember? You said you couldn't figure out what had gone wrong—why you were still waiting for your ship to come in and how you should have majored in premed instead of banking."

"I do not carry on, Maura. Not about anything. Children carry on."

"As if," Maura mumbled.

"I simply pointed out a few of the negative aspects of deciduous trees and made a suggestion based on sound economical principles that we save money by using them to feed our fireplace come winter rather than paying to have logs delivered, that's all."

Maura rolled her eyes. "Whatever. You must have liked it okay once you got out there, though."

Jason looked at his daughter in surprise. "What makes you say that?"

"You went over and helped Catherine with hers once we were done," Maura pointed out. "And then you went back and took the shovel right out of her hand so you could dig holes for her tulips."

"I did not."

"Yes you did. I was watching out the window. Dad?"

First Catherine, now Maura. Was every female he knew determined to drive him wacko today? Had he really taken the shovel out of Catherine's hand? He didn't remember. It didn't matter. He had several reports to work on before he could go to bed, and he'd already wasted a major portion of the afternoon helping Miss Manic Depressive next door.

Jason drew a deep breath, determined to hang on to his patience, but it was getting more and more slippery as the day went on. "What?"

"We haven't planted any flowers or bulbs since I came to stay with you, and if you planted any before that, they didn't work. Don't you think our house is going to look pretty stupid when all Catherine's tulips come up and we have nothing?"

Jason shook his head. "Oh, no, you don't. I'm just getting the use of my fingers back now. I am not going back outside to freeze them off again. Besides, it's after five and it's Sunday. I'm sure all the stores are closed. Where would we get the bulbs to plant?"

Maura frowned. "I guess we'll have to wait for that, then—but Dad?"

Jason was immediately back on alert. Hell, he'd thought he was in the clear for a second or two there. He should have known better. "What?"

"We have the blue paint for my bedroom in the basement. It's been down there for six months."

"Maura, honey—"

"You painted Catherine's nursery for her, and I know you had a good time. You were smiling and laughing the whole time."

"That was different." Catherine had been there. She'd looked adorable with her hair all stuck up inside a baseball-style cap and yellow spatters on her face. How was he supposed to not have smiled? "Homework," Jason said, feeling a bit desperate. "Don't you have any assignments you need to get done for tomorrow?"

Maura crossed her arms over her budding bosom and tapped her foot. "You did it for her, Dad. Aren't I just as important?"

"Of course you are. Music. Don't you have to practice for your flute lesson?"

"Dad—"

Jason knew when he was beat. He went down to the basement to get the can of blue paint, knowing full well he'd be buying up dribs and drabs of tulip bulbs wherever he could still find any to plant next weekend to keep Maura happy.

This was all that woman's fault.

Chapter Nine

Jason spent the next week desperately trying to understand the changes he felt happening in his personal life. He drove around the area taking photos of homes that had recently sold in the same price range as the one he was working up an appraisal on. The flower beds surrounding the homes with their frost-dead arrangements reminded him of how he himself had felt dead inside after the dissolution of his marriage. Realizing just how dead he'd been for so long made his preoccupation with his new next-door neighbor all the more amazing to him. If only he could take the position of an impartial observer, he was sure he'd be fascinated by it.

Unfortunately he was living the scenario, not observing it—and living it was damned uncomfortable. Jason thought it might be rather like when your foot or your arm fell asleep. When the circulation finally returned to the area, it felt like pins and needles and hurt like hell for a while. His psyche had pins and needles right then. It hurt like hell every time Catherine came to mind.

It was a good analogy. He liked it. Jason nodded to himself as he swung into his driveway that afternoon. He planned to work on the comparables in his home office, but his mind wasn't on real estate. He just wished he knew what to do about his fascination with Catherine. She gave him a headache. She was crazy. Would it be better to seek her out? Overdose on her company, provided she'd even speak to him right now? Or should he simply treat her like an addiction and try to quit cold turkey, avoid her whenever possible?

"Maura," he called as he came in the back door. "I'm home."

There was no answer. Jason laid his briefcase on the countertop and set the bag of four dozen mixed spring bulbs he'd managed to find on top of it. Catherine's house would be all color coordinated come May. Jason was afraid his was going to look like a crazy quilt. But Maura would be pleased, and that counted for something.

He paused, listening. There was no music off in the distance, no television blasting from the family room. No reason at all for Maura not to hear him and respond.

"Maura?" The two of them hadn't had words that morning. She wouldn't be ignoring him out of pique. Jason felt panic begin to claw at his insides. School had let out forty-five minutes ago. Damn it, she should be here by now. "Maura! Baby, where are you?"

This did it, Jason told himself as he flew into the front hall. He didn't care how old she was, he was arranging for some kind of after-school thing. A check-in with a neighbor—something. She'd done this once before, where she'd forgotten to leave a note, and Jason was sure he'd lost a couple of years off his life before he'd tracked her down. Damn it, he'd told her he was coming home early.

Jason checked the family room and living room. Both empty. He checked the dining room, although why she'd be in a room they'd yet to use he couldn't imagine. Empty again.

Jason started up the stairs, calling Maura's name all the way. He said something a lot stronger than "Oh fiddlesticks." He was too worried to enjoy finally cutting loose after years of watching himself in front of his daughter.

Maura had sworn she was walking home on the opposite side of the street now, walking against traffic. She probably wasn't. She'd probably been kidnapped. It was the only logical answer. God knew she was far and away the prettiest seventh-grader in that entire pimple-stricken junior high. Any child molester with any taste or discretion at all would choose her, there was no doubt in Jason's mind of that.

"Maura!" There was a desperate edge to his voice now.

Jason came to a dead stop at the top of the stairs. He tilted his head to the right and listened. There. What was that?

"Daddy? I'm in here."

There was a hitch in his daughter's voice. And hiccups. Yes, definitely hiccups. "I hate it when you do that, honey," Jason said while he leaned against the banister for support. Relief had sapped the strength right out of his legs. "What room are you in? Where's 'here'?" He listened again, determined to get a fix on his daughter's voice this time. She was upset over something; he was willing to put money on it. He'd also bet she'd been crying.

Anger brought the starch back to his muscles. He stood up straight and clenched his fists. Honest to God, if those little locker-room monsters had been at her again, he would personally—

"The bathroom, Dad. I'm in the bathroom."

The voice was faint, wavering, but definitely the correct direction for the room in question. Jason moved down the hall to the right door. It was closed. So Jason stood there and talked to the wooden panel. "Sweetheart? Is anything wrong?"

"Oh, Daddy!" It was muffled by the closed door, but Jason would have had to have been deaf to miss the anguish in Maura's wail.

He jiggled the knob. Locked. "What? What!" Jason raked his hand through his hair, leaving it standing on end in his agitation. Adolescents should come with instructions, some kind of manual. Parents of newborns learned to differentiate the various types of cries; could the same be done for the wailing of teenagers? And would he, poor inadequate male that he was, would he ever master the skill? Jason could hear her sobbing through the door, but he had no idea if she'd broken a nail or every bone in her body. Maura would treat either as a major calamity. He was determined to ferret out the problem and if at all possible, fix things to the best of his ability for his daughter.

"Maura, just tell me this. Do I need to call the doctor?"

"I don't think so."

"You don't *think* so? You're not sure? Maura, I'm not leaving this spot until I get a coherent explanation of what's wrong with you."

"Oh, Daddy!" his daughter wailed once more.

"Stop that," he ordered, both from fear and frustration. Once more, Jason futilely jiggled the handle. "Tell me what's wrong. I can't come up with the solution if you don't define the problem for me. Maura?"

But his daughter only cried harder, if he was to judge by the increase in the decibel level of her hiccups. "That does it," Jason announced. "Open this door right now. If you don't open this door *this very second*, I'm going to break it down. Do you hear me, Maura? I'm going to kick the da—darn door in." Trying to watch his language while dealing with his daughter was going to leave him with a permanent stutter, Jason decided. Damn it, anyway.

"No," Maura shrieked. "Don't do that. Please, Daddy, don't do that."

You'd have thought Jason made a habit of kicking things in just to terrorize his daughter the way Maura was carrying on now. Thoroughly exasperated and thoroughly scared, Jason pleaded with the closed door. "Baby, I'm trying to help you, but you are not cooperating. I can't fulfil my fatherly function when you refuse to open the door so I can see what's wrong. Now are you going to open it or not?" It hurt to be reasonable. It physically hurt. His stomach ached, and the muscles in his arms and shoulders were so tight Jason figured he'd have permanent knots.

"Get Catherine, okay, Daddy? Go get Catherine. Tell her I need her."

Jason's head snapped back as though his face had been slapped. In fact, that was just how he felt. His daughter was in pain and once again refusing his aid. She preferred to confide in some next-door neighbor she'd known for only a couple of weeks. Some *insane* next-door neighbor.

"Is this about your underwear again?" he asked suspiciously.

"No. Daddy, please?"

Jason was about at the end of his rope. He hadn't had a cigarette since he'd first read about the dangers of secondhand smoke and begun to worry about Maura. That had been eight years ago. He'd kill for one right then. He hooked his thumbs through the loops of his slacks and strove for patience. "Honey, Catherine's at work. It's barely four o'clock. She won't be home for another hour and a half. Be reasonable. Just open the door."

That logical explanation was not well received. In fact, it was met with nothing but dead silence.

Jason began pacing in front of the bathroom door. Two steps this way, then two steps that. "Maura? Honey? Say something so I'll know you're still alive in there. Can't you just tell me the problem? I'm your father. I'll fix it for you, I swear I will or I'll die trying."

"Really?"

Now he was insulted. She needed to ask? Jason stared at the door. "Of course, really."

More silence.

"Daddy?"

"Yes?"

"Could you call Amy for me?"

"Call Amy?" he repeated, befuddled. "What for? And you're going to have to unlock the door to talk to Amy anyhow. Unless you want me to hold the receiver up to door so the two of you can yell at each other."

"No, you talk to her. Tell her, tell her to call Catherine at the shop and say I need some—"

"Some what?" This better be good, Jason told himself as he stripped off his jacket and slung it over the banister, then followed it up with his tie. He rolled up his shirtsleeves. He was now prepared to fight his daughter's demons. Unfortunately, given that daughter's total lack of cooperation and faith in her father, he had absolutely no idea as to the identity of the enemy. Jason raked his hand through his hair once more.

"Um, tell her to tell Catherine that I need some—some of what Miss Jackson talked about last week in class. She'll know what I mean."

Oh, for crying out loud. "You hope," Jason muttered. If Amy was half as ditzy as his own darling daughter God only knew what she'd conclude Maura was in need of. Catherine could show up with—just about anything. "Maura, who is Miss Jackson?"

"She's the gym teacher. Also skills for living."

"Uh-huh. The gym teacher." He knew it. It was those damn locker-room witches at it again. "What do you need? A different brand of gym shoes? Is the kind we bought last week not 'in' enough? Did you split your gym shorts? You can tell me that. That's not so bad. We'll just get another pair. Umbros this time, if you want.''

"Daddy, please just call Amy and say—say what I said to say.''

Jason threw up his arms and shook his head. "Okay, fine. I'll call Amy and tell her you need some of whatever Miss Jackson has in gym class. I just hope you end up with something even remotely resembling whatever it is you're having a fit about. And you'll have to keep talking to me through the door the entire time we wait, do you hear me, young lady? I want to be sure you don't do something stupid like pass out in there from loss of blood or something. You didn't cut yourself, did you? If you need stitches and aren't telling me, I'll probably brain you once I get my hands on you. Really give the doctor something to sew up.''

"I don't need stitches, Daddy.''

"All right. I'm going to go make the call, even though I'll feel like a total idiot. You start singing or reciting the pledge of allegiance. The minute I stop hearing your voice is the minute I break the door down, you hear me?''

"Yes, Daddy.''

Jason grunted. She better believe it, too. He was dead serious.

Maura was down to eighteen bottles of beer on the wall, and Jason had settled in on the top step, his head propped on his fist when Catherine finally arrived. There was a peremptory knock on the door, but no pause for admission. Catherine walked right in after the brief warning. Amy trailed after her.

"Jason? Maura? We're here."

Jason hauled himself off the step. "Up here, Catherine. Hey, Amy, I didn't realize you were coming, too."

"Oh, I wouldn't miss this for the world. Not once you told me what had happened. This is so exciting. I want Maura to tell me all about it. How it feels. Everything."

Catherine glanced up the staircase and smiled at the frazzled picture Jason made. He obviously had yet to figure out what was ailing his daughter. She almost smiled, but thought better of it. Jason did not look in a mood to share a bit of humor.

"Amy, go on out into the kitchen and heat up some cider. Mr. Engel looks like he could use a cup, and I bet Maura will want some, too."

Jason grunted. "What are you going to do, pour it under the door? She won't unlock it."

"Aunt Cath, I want to stay with you and talk to Maura—"

"You can interview her later. Scat."

Amy reluctantly took herself off. Catherine started up the stairs. "I'll get her to open it, Jason, but you're going to have give up your vigil by the door if I'm to succeed."

"Why? If she's sick, I need to be here."

Catherine had reached him by then. She put her finger to her lips, then opened the top of the bag she clutched and held it so that Jason could see its contents.

He gasped. His eyes rolled in his head until, greatly widened, they stared at the bathroom door. "Not Maura. Not my baby."

Catherine nodded sympathetically. "'Fraid so."

"She's too young," He whispered back, shock evident in his voice.

She wondered if he knew he'd covered his heart with his hand, as though to protect it from the shock. "I was exactly the same age."

"You were? Twelve?"

Catherine nodded seriously. She wanted to laugh. Maybe someday Jason would see the humor in the situation, but she doubted it would be today. She bit her bottom lip instead.

Jason sat down heavily on the top step once more. He rubbed his face with his hands. "I can't believe it. My little girl. First brassieres and now this. I can't stand it." He looked up at Catherine. "This," he said solemnly, "is why a girl needs a mother and a boy needs a father. This is a perfect illustration of what I was trying to explain to you the other day. What if you get yourself pregnant and have a little boy? Who'd take him shopping for his first jockstrap when he started playing sports?" He sighed. "Well, give me the pads and tell me what she's supposed to do with them. I'll try and explain it. God knows how I'll manage to get through this without mortifying us both half to death." Jason looked thunderstruck. "Her first period. You know what this means, Catherine?"

Catherine smiled. "She's a woman?"

"It means she's capable of getting pregnant, that's what it means." Jason smacked his forehead. "Boys. There will be boys coming around. It's only a matter of time before they notice how she's developing. I'll have to get a shotgun. They don't need to know there won't be any bullets in it. Just something to intimidate the hell out of them.''

"Jason, that's ridiculous. You're overreacting." He looked mortally insulted, but Catherine refused to take it back. "Now if you're anything like my brothers, you'll never be able to pull this off and that's okay. That's why I'm here. I'll deal with Maura. You go down to the kitchen with Amy. We'll be right there. Have the cider ready."

"She's my daughter," he said, staying.

Catherine listened to Maura go from the beer bottle song to "Mary Had a Little Lamb" without even so much as a hitch, evidently believing her father's threat to kick down the door if she stopped making noise. Did either one of them have any idea how ludicrous this entire scene was? Catherine smiled to herself. The two of them were absolutely adorable together. Jason especially. He tried so hard, but Maura's adolescence was simply beyond him. What a sweetheart. She forgot all about how irritated she was with him.

Catherine patted his arm. "I know, Jason, but this is better done by a woman. Trust me."

Catherine took her bag of supplies and knocked on the bathroom door. "Maura? It's me, Catherine."

You could hear her break out into fresh sobs. "Thanks for coming, Catherine. I didn't know what else to do."

"It's fine, sweetheart, just fine. Business was slow today. I just closed a little early. No problem. Now open the door. I've got the stuff."

"Is Daddy gone?"

Catherine turned and raised an eyebrow at Jason in a see-I-told-you-so kind of expression. For a moment she thought he was going to refuse to leave, but finally, reluctantly, he sighed and started slowly down the steps. Catherine knew how hard it was for him to leave this to her. It made him all the more dear to her.

"Yes, honey. He's leaving."

Maura waited another few seconds, then Catherine heard the latch pop. The door opened a cautious three inches. All Catherine saw was a single eyeball centered between a sliver of forehead and cheek. This age group was so amusing. How could Jason not laugh? It was probably as Monica always told her, it was a whole lot funnier when they belonged to somebody else.

"He's really gone?"

"Yes."

"Catherine, I just couldn't tell him. I couldn't. I was going to try and call you, then wait in the downstairs bathroom, but I heard his car in the driveway and so I ran real quick and locked myself in here."

Catherine soothed her. "It's all right, Maura. He'll get over his hurt. He's your father and he loves you. He understands. At least he's trying to. Do you want me to hand you the bag or do you want me to come in there with you?"

A hand snaked out the narrow opening. "I'll take the bag."

"Here you go, Maura. You need me to show you what to do or anything?"

"No. Miss Jackson took all the girls aside and explained everything to us."

"That's good, sweetie," Catherine said. "And now that your dad knows you're a woman, he'll buy them for you and you can just keep them in the bathroom for whenever you need them.''

"Thanks, Catherine. Thanks a lot.''

"You're welcome, kiddo. Come on down when you're ready.''

Catherine made it halfway down the stairs before the giggles got her. Clamping her mouth shut, she made it the rest of the way down and almost to the kitchen before she succumbed. Not wanting Maura to hear, she hurried. Catherine didn't want Maura to misinterpret. It was the situation, not the child. Jason had looked ready to pull his hair out when she'd arrived. Maura, hit over the head by incipient womanhood, had been so sweet in her confusion and modesty. Oh, God. The two of them together were a recipe for disaster at this stage in their lives. Catherine sat in a kitchen chair and began to laugh.

"What in the world is the matter with you?'' Jason asked after sharing an amazed look with Amy. The two of them then stared at Catherine, convinced she'd completely flipped her lid.

"Aunt Cath, this is *not* funny,'' Amy primly informed her. "It's a momentous event in a young girl's life.''

"Right.'' Catherine sagged back in the chair. "Absolutely.'' She managed to get herself back under control, but when she looked at Jason, she lost it again. The look on his face when she'd shown him the bag of pads—she promptly doubled over again.

"Aunt Cath—''

Catherine sat back again and wiped her eyes. "Sorry, honey. I'll sober up, I promise. I'm sure it's highly insulting to your tender young ego, but sometimes your age group is too cute for words. You and Maura are the best. Absolutely the best.''

Jason slumped into the chair next to her. Tipping his head in her direction, he asked, ''Am I a lot grayer?''

''Nah,'' Catherine said after only a cursory inspection. Then she was hit by a giggle aftershock. Once it receded, she passed the question along to Amy. ''What do you think, Amy?''

Amy took Jason's concerns more seriously. ''I'm not sure,'' she said, studying Jason's head thoughtfully. ''It's been a couple of weeks, after all, and I can't exactly remember how gray it was to start with.''

Jason growled again, and Catherine was hit by another laughter tremor. ''Oh, man, I'm going to kill myself before I get out of here.''

''You won't have to,'' Jason grumbled. ''I'll do the job for you, if you don't stop laughing at me.''

''Not at you, Jason,'' Catherine corrected. ''Never at you. Just *with* you, that's the only way I'll ever laugh.''

''Seeing as how I'm not laughing at the moment, that's a little difficult to believe.''

Catherine rose, picked up all three mugs and carried them to the sink. ''Oh, but you need to start seeing the humor in all this, Jason. It's the only way you'll maintain your sanity over the next eight to ten years.''

Jason winced and reached for the cigarettes that hadn't been there for years. Eight to ten years. It sounded like a prison sentence to him. Maura was an intelligent girl. Surely if he applied reason and logic he'd be able to get her to see the foolishness of this adolescent garbage. No child of his would need eight to ten years to wallow in this silliness that was slowly driving him up a wall. Surely not.

Chapter Ten

"Good morning, you've reached Hand Arounds. This is Catherine speaking."

"Catherine, this is Jason. Jason Engel. You're probably busy, so I won't keep you, but I wanted to tell you thank you one more time for everything you did yesterday."

Catherine smiled into her telephone. She couldn't help it. He'd been so damn cute yesterday, so totally clueless. She moved a box of straight pins to the other side of the cash register and shifted a roll of sticky dots into the vacated place. "Jason, the flowers and the bag of candy Maura brought over last night were more than sufficient thanks. I can't remember the last time I've seen such a variety of candy bars. What did you do, buy one of everything?"

"I wasn't sure what your favorite kind was."

"I have several, actually, and you hit every one of them."

"Oh, well, good then."

Catherine heard him inhale. She opened the side of the cash register and checked the tape, then straightened out a spindle of receipts. Jason cleared his throat. Catherine almost sighed out loud. She had a very clear picture in her mind's eye. He was so sexy and so incredibly adorable when he was ill at ease.

"Well, I guess I'll let you go. Oh, I almost forgot. You need to let me know how much you spent on the, um, pads so I can reimburse you."

"Don't worry about it, Jason. My treat."

"Oh, no. Call me old-fashioned, but I pay for my own daughter's personal items."

Catherine laughed. "Fine. Be that way. Three bucks should cover it. Everything's all right now with Maura?"

Jason sighed. "Other than the fact that she's not speaking to me? Yes, everything's all right."

Catherine rearranged her pens, glad for once that the store was empty. It allowed her to give her full attention to Jason. "Why isn't she talking to you?"

"Because I told her that on the days when I couldn't work out of the house in the afternoon, we were going to have to find somebody she could check in with when she got home from school, starting right now. I've got afternoon appointments twice this week that I can't break, so I'm going to start calling around today. That makes me mean in her eyes. On top of which, I treat her like she's still a baby. I don't trust her. I don't have any faith in her ability to take care of herself. Oh, yes, and she wishes she'd never been born because her life might as well be over if I make her do this, especially if it's the lady across the street with the two-year-old twins. She'll probably try to make her baby-sit or treat her like a two-year-old, she wasn't sure which, but whatever it was, it was sure to be loathsome."

"All of that? Wow." Catherine sifted paper clips with one hand while she thought. Why should she be nice to Jason who was denying her her fondest dream? On the other hand, why cut off her nose to spite her face? She thought Maura was funny and really enjoyed her company. "Jason? Why don't you just let her come here those two days? She can do her homework in the back room and there's a small TV there she can watch when she's done with that. If she really gets bored, she can help me tag clothes."

"No, Catherine. This isn't your problem. Maura will just have to—"

"Jason, I wouldn't have offered if I minded. Seriously, Amy does it all the time. That's why I have the TV back there. She won't be any trouble."

"Well—"

"It's settled then. Tell her I'll see her, when?"

"Tuesday and Thursday."

"Right. Tell her I'll see her then."

Jason brought Catherine more flowers when he picked up Maura on Tuesday. Catherine was touched.

"Everything went all right?" he asked as Maura packed up her backpack.

"Yeah, sure. We had a little bit of trouble with the one math problem with trains starting at opposite ends of the line, one going seventy miles per hour and the other sixty miles per hour. For some strange reason, the book wanted to know when they'd meet up. One would only hope they were on separate tracks and wouldn't meet at all, but we figured it out all right. I think.''

"You helped her with her math?''

Catherine smiled at the bouquet of mums she was arranging in a glass. "Like I said, it got a little rocky on the one problem, but other than that Maura sailed right through them. She's really quite bright, Jason.''

"Yes, I know.'' Jason shook his head, not knowing what to make of the fact that Catherine sounded like a proud mother.

"Just so you know, she practiced her flute for twenty-five minutes. I timed it. She said you'd say that was enough.''

It was more than Jason was usually able to get out of her. "She practiced here? For twenty-five minutes?''

"Yeah. These three little kids who were in here with their moms were positively fascinated. I don't know much about music, but I'd be willing to bet Maura's got a lot of talent.''

Jason was dazed. "I've always thought so,'' he said.

Thursday was much the same. Jason spoke to Maura about it during the car trip home from Hand Arounds.

"So,'' he began, "you and Catherine got along all right?''

"Yeah, sure, Dad. She's pretty cool. I mean, the hemline on her skirt needs some serious attention. She needs to lose about six inches off the bottom there, and her hair could maybe use a perm or maybe some blond streaks. Yeah, that's it. She needs to streak her hair.''

Jason turned a corner and glanced over at his daughter, appalled. ''She does not. Her hair is beautiful just the way it is. Don't you dare tell her to streak it. You might hurt her feelings.''

''Daaad, credit me with a brain, okay?'' Maura shrugged. ''I know enough not to hurt her feelings. Anyway, other than that, she's pretty okay. Did you know she can do 'work story' problems? The hard kind where so and so works by himself painting a house for an hour at such and such a rate, then some other guy starts helping him only he can't work as fast, so how long will it take to finish painting the house? She can figure that all out. Too bad we didn't think to time how fast you could plant tulip bulbs, then how fast Catherine could. If we'd only done that, I bet Catherine could have predicted exactly how long it would have taken to get them all in. Then I'd have known exactly when to start the cider so it would be all ready and waiting.''

''Catherine's amazing.'' But lest his daughter not appreciate all the help he'd given her over the past year and a half, ''I can do story problems too, you know, Maura. And as for those bulbs, I was just a little too busy planting the stupid things to worry about the timing of the thing. Heck, if I'd stopped long enough to figure out what the exact length of the task was going to be, I'd have frozen to death before I ever got the first one in. But I could have if I'd wanted to, kiddo.''

''Yeah, but you weren't there today, were you?''

No. He hadn't been there to figure out when the

painters would finish their task. Catherine was the one his daughter turned to more and more frequently. He was grateful. He was impressed. He was also jealous as heck.

Maura stayed with Catherine after school once the following week and twice the week after that. By then Christmas was breathing down their necks and the home-appraisal business was fairly slow. Jason had a lot of time to think about his situation. In fact, on December nineteenth, when he should have been concentrating on the Christmas gift list in front of him—it still had several alarming blank spots after some key names, Catherine being one of them—he found himself doing just that. Again.

His pen poised over the empty spot by Catherine's name, Jason tried to concentrate on gift options. It was tough. Catherine refused payment for keeping tabs on Maura, insisting it was her pleasure, but Jason hadn't been comfortable with that. He'd been very careful to bring her a nice, but not so nice as to be embarrassing, gift after each Maura sitting job. Generic, nonpersonal little things.

"But I should still get her something extra special," he told himself. "She's really gone above and beyond just being a good neighbor." And it wasn't just that, he admitted to himself. Catherine herself was unique in his eyes, and she'd never asked for anything in return—except for the one thing he was totally uncomfortable providing.

Perfume? No. Not special enough. She already smelled fantastic, anyway.

"Maura really relates well to Catherine and she seems to understand the workings of the adolescent mind which is quite a feat.'' And Catherine had gone to a great deal of trouble to fix up her back room so that Amy and now Maura would be comfortable when they came. It was a lot of work to go through for the occasional visitor. Catherine seemed to genuinely like it when the girls stopped by. She even kept after-school snacks ready for them.

Some kind of lingerie? Not if he wanted his heart to keep beating. He still got an occasional chest pain, thinking about that twenty-eight-dollar bra she'd confessed to owning.

He concentrated on how Catherine had somehow slid perfectly into an unknown groove in his life. He and Maura limped by. They could manage if they had to. But that was what it was—managing. Catherine provided sunshine. She was the tulips in their lives. She made Maura smile. She made Jason do more than smile. She made him swear in frustration at all the feelings that bubbled up in him. Male feelings. Man stuff. Yeah, she made him laugh, she ticked him off, and she eased his life while she complicated it. But primarily Catherine made him hot. Just thinking about how hot Catherine could make him had Jason shrugging out of his sweatshirt and rolling up the sleeves of the long-sleeved shirt he wore.

"Damn," he muttered.

Sometimes when he walked in to pick up Maura, Catherine would be behind her counter, working her register with a pencil stuck behind her ear, an ink smudge on her cheek, and a look of total concentration on her face. Jason would study her without her being aware. It was probably the smudge on her flawless complexion that did him in, he thought when he tried to get analytical. But whatever it was, at times like those, he felt hot enough to self-combust.

"Maura?"

"Yeah, Dad?"

"Check the thermostat, will you, honey? It feels awfully warm in here."

He knew what he really felt like getting her. Something that would give him some claim to wiping off that smudge like, say a diamond ring. More and more lately, he wanted her around permanently. This having to track her down every time he wanted to discuss something, be it Maura or the state of the Union was for the birds. He wanted to be able to turn to her and say it. She should be right there waiting for his pearls of wisdom. But marriage? He chewed the top of his pen. That was totally impossible, of course. Wasn't it?

Of course it was. Catherine wanted a baby, Jason didn't. Instant impasse.

Or was it?

Jason mulled the possibility over. Catherine was becoming more and more attached to Maura; that was obvious to even the most casual observer. Not that that was any big surprise, Maura was, after all, a superior child. Beautiful, smart, talented. Several weeks had gone by since Catherine had asked him to give her a baby. Maybe things had changed. Maybe she'd formed enough of an attachment to him and Maura that she'd be willing to adopt them as her family and forego the pain of childbirth.

It was a possibility.

His eyes went out of focus as he stared at the paper in front of him and thought.

He'd never realized until Catherine moved in next door how all alone he'd been since his divorce. He kind of thought, from the amount of time she let Maura spend with her, that Catherine might be lonely, too. There was no doubt in his mind that they'd be sexually compatible. Either she was severely asthmatic or her rising passions had interfered with her breathing, just as much as his had the few times the flames of passion he tried so hard to keep banked had flared up. Both of their lungs had been working like bellows in those instances.

Most importantly, he genuinely liked her as a person, and Jason thought that was reciprocated. Seemed to him it was a win-win deal for the two of them. She got Maura and him and he and Maura got her.

So why the hell not?

Jason looked back down at his list. He threw the pen down and muttered, "Forget Grandma Fay and the president of the bank, even if he does sign my paycheck. I'll think of something for them later. Right now I want to go to the jewelry store in the mall and look at rings."

On the evening of the twenty-fourth, he tucked it into his shirt pocket, crunched through the crisp top of the snow on his way across their backyards and knocked on her back door. He was nervous, yes, but somehow sure that he was on the right course.

Catherine answered in a thick robe and fur-lined plaid slippers. Obviously she'd been planning an early night. "Hi, Jason. This is a surprise. Where's Maura?"

"She's making her Christmas visit to her mother, but she'll be home early in the morning to spend

Christmas with me. I came over tonight because there's something I want to talk to you about without her around.''

Catherine blinked but invited him in. That was a good sign, wasn't it? She had to know it was going to be personal if he didn't want his daughter to hear.

He came into the kitchen. Catherine studied him expectantly. "Uh, could we maybe sit down somewhere?"

"What? Oh, sure. Let's go in the living room."

Catherine plugged in the tree, sat on the sofa and looked up expectantly.

"I have another gift at home for you," he said. "Maura and I will bring it over sometime tomorrow."

"Better make it in the late morning or early afternoon. I'll be at church for nine-thirty services then to five-o'clock supper at Monica's."

"Fine. We'll stop by around one."

"I have some gifts for you two, as well. I'll give them to you then."

"Okay."

They stared at each other silently for a moment. Jason was first to break eye contact. He moved over to look out the living room window. There was absolutely nothing to see in the pitch-dark. He glanced back over at Catherine. It was now or never. "Catherine," he said. "Let's sit down for a minute. There's something I want to talk to you about."

"I am sitting down."

"Yes, you are. Well I'm going to sit down, then." And he did. Right next to her. He took one of her hands into his and played with her fingers. Jason then proceeded to take her through the same line of reasoning he'd used to convince himself of how a marriage between the two of them could work out to everyone's mutual advantage. He did it all without ever once looking up from their entwined hands. When Jason finished, he breathed a sigh of relief, proud of the way he'd held his voice steady and refrained from stuttering during his presentation. He just hoped Catherine appreciated how hard it was for him to even think along the lines of commitment again. Well, he was almost done.

All those tiny little lights on the Christmas tree must throw an incredible amount of heat, he was thinking. It was suddenly sweltering in there. He used the sleeve of his flannel shirt to wipe his forehead, then fished the ring box out of his pocket and put it in her hand. "Look at it," he urged. "My eyes were crossing by the time I was done trying to find just the right one. It's like you. Simple, understated, but when you really take the time to look, full of fire. Beautiful."

Catherine was nothing less than stunned. She stared at the small velvety box in her palm. "Let me get this straight," she said slowly. "You want to marry me? Because I'm good with Maura and you and I get along okay? We're compatible? Define *in every way* for me, please."

Maybe *compatible* hadn't been a good choice for what he was feeling, but he was a real estate appraiser, for God's sake, not some kind of wordsmith. Jason eyed Catherine warily. He couldn't help but notice that she still hadn't so much as glanced inside the ring box. No. In fact, she was looking at the small gray velvet square container as though it might suddenly grow fangs and attack. Something told him he might be in trouble here.

"Now, Catherine, I didn't mean to make it sound as though getting married would simply make things more convenient all the way around. No, there's more to it than that."

"What?"

"Uh—"

"That's what I thought. Jason, I've come to love Maura as if she were my own, but I'm not going to do what you're asking just so I can have a child. All these years I've wanted a baby damn badly, but I never married just so I could get one." Tears flooded her eyes. She scrubbed them away with the backs of her hands.

She stood and went over to the tree. She closely examined one of the heirloom ornaments her mother had given her when she'd moved into her first apartment. That painted glass bell that tinkled so lightly when she nudged it with a finger had been on every tree she'd ever known and some she hadn't from the years before her birth. That bell and the small handful of others like it, sprinkled throughout the tree, meant a lot to her, represented a lot. Her parents' love and devotion to each other and their determination to provide memories for their children even during the lean-year Christmases hit her right in the face every year when she hung those bells. That's what she wanted for herself, she suddenly realized. The baby she'd craved for so long was a symptom of the larger need. Holy cow, she thought, stunned by the revelation.

She turned to Jason, leaving the bell tinkling madly and looked him right in the face. "Compatible, con-

venient, a way with kids—those are all such lukewarm appellations when compared to undying love,
unfailing devotion and total commitment, don't you
think? I'm worth more, Jason, and I've only just realized it. I'll go without rather than settle for less."

Catherine tucked the ring case she still clutched
into Jason's palm. She curled his unresistant fingers
around it, then let her hand drop away. "Thanks for
the offer, Jason. A week or two ago I'd have probably
jumped at it, and we'd both have been cheated. Bring
Maura over tomorrow. I bought a bunch of stuff for
her I think she'll really like."

Jason sat there for a moment, obviously stunned.
Finally he nodded and tucked the ring case back into
his pocket. He rose, looked over his shoulder at Catherine and shook his head as if not able to discern what
had just happened. Finally he left, a disappointed expression on his face.

After he'd gone, Catherine went up to the nursery
she'd so lovingly decorated. She sat in the dark in the
bentwood rocker and rocked for a long time. Many
times over the next two weeks she returned to that
rocker. She would rock in the dark and contemplate
her life, its meaning, its cosmic significance. Did it
have any? Who knew?

Monica called with news the week after New
Year's Eve. "My next-door neighbor told me she
thinks she's pregnant. She's got an ob appointment
day after tomorrow. Amy's going to sit for her while
she goes. Want me to have her ask about a sperm
bank for an anonymous friend? She's pretty bold. She
just painted her front door orange. She'd do it."

What a question. Too bad she didn't have an answer. Here was her opportunity to get everything she used to think she wanted. But even if she got pregnant now, would just a baby be enough, now that she'd fallen for both Jason and his daughter? Why couldn't he love her? Why?

"Catherine? You hear me?"

Suddenly Catherine knew the answer. She'd been avoiding it for two weeks, not wanting to completely give up her dreams and be left with nothing. "No," she said, surprising herself with the firmness of her decision. "Don't bother. I've decided not to go that route after all."

Monica gasped. "What?"

"What, what? You should be relieved. I've decided you're right. A baby should be the product of two people in love. Prince Charming might be taken, but I'm going to wait around a while longer and see if his brother shows up." He already had. He was living next door but she wasn't about to admit to Monica that she'd been right all along. Not yet. "Meanwhile, I'm going to dismantle this crib, take it back to the shop and use this room for a study, I think. I'll throw myself into my job and quit wasting time worrying over what I don't have."

"But, Cath—"

"Oh, there's the doorbell," she lied, not willing to argue with her sister. "I've got to hang up. I'll get back to you, okay, Monica?"

Catherine could hear her sister's frustrated wail as she replaced the receiver, but she hardened her heart. Catherine went back upstairs to the nursery. This time she turned on the light when she entered the room. She studied the crib for a long time.

There was only one baby she wanted. Jason's.

Why? Because she loved Jason. Unfortunately those feelings were not reciprocated, and even if they were, she realized she loved him too much to pressure him into doing something he really wasn't comfortable with. Ergo, no baby for Catherine. All of this self-realization stuff left her with only one choice, which was ridiculous. If there was only one, it wasn't a choice, was it? Catherine sighed. She would mourn the loss of her unknown child, but she'd also get on with things. It would be hard when her very livelihood revolved around baby things, but she could do it. She *would* do it.

The first step was often the most difficult, and it was best to get it done. Catherine went to retrieve a screwdriver. She would take the crib back to the shop and sell it. She could do this, maybe not with a heck of a lot of grace, but she could do it.

Catherine cried herself to sleep that night.

Five days later Maura came to see her in the store. "Hi, Catherine. Dad has to drive around and take more pictures of houses for comparables and I don't want to go. I think he's afraid I'm going to lock myself in the bathroom again if I stay home by myself. So, is it all right if I stay here? I can help you tag clothes if you want. None of my teachers assigned any homework tonight. Isn't that awesome? Hey, isn't that the crib from your house? What's it doing here?"

"Oh, well, I uh—" Suddenly she was blinking back tears. Catherine turned around so Maura wouldn't notice them and bumped right into Jason.

"Oh!" she cried, and put her hand over her chest

to pat her heart. "Give me a heart attack, why don't you?"

"I was waiting out in the car for Maura to come back and tell me if it was okay for her to stay here for a little while," he explained uncomfortably. "Then I noticed that." He pointed to her window display. "Catherine?"

She was still preoccupied with calming her heart palpitations. "What?"

"That's the crib out of your nursery, isn't it?"

No point denying the obvious. "Yes, it is. I've decided to be realistic about things. Somebody ought to get some use out of the thing, and since it's not going to be me, I decided to sell it. How's that for maturity? No more living in a dreamworld for me, no sirree, Bob. From now on I deal with life exactly how it is and where I find myself in it." And it was killing her.

Jason left Hand Arounds a few minutes later, feeling about par with a slug. He knew how much Catherine had wanted a baby. It had been in her expression when she'd literally immersed herself in baby paraphernalia at the rummage sale that long-ago Saturday morning. It had shone from her eyes when she'd gathered up all her courage to ask him if he'd father one for her. It had been obvious in the pleased tilt of her chin when she'd glanced around the nursery she'd created to bring her child home to. He'd only been fooling himself when he'd thought she might have gotten over it the night he'd decided to propose.

Jason groaned as he drove around the area snapping pictures of several recently sold three-bedroom ranch homes. "She's completely given up her dreams," he complained to himself in disbelief. "Why?" Jason pulled over to the side of the road and parked to contemplate the question. "Never mind the why, *how* can she do it? She wanted it so badly. She must really be crushed, and I did that to her. Me." He pulled a half-eaten roll of Life Savers from the glove compartment that Maura must have left there and began to demolish them, one right after the other while he puzzled things through.

Was he just being egotistical, accepting all the blame here? No, he didn't think so. Catherine had seemed different for a while now, and it appeared to him that the turning point had come right around the time he'd refused her request to father her baby. "What does that tell me?" he asked the empty car as he crunched through the last hard cherry candy. He crumpled the empty candy papers into his hand and stuffed them into the door handle's little trash receptacle. "It tells me that it was my baby or nothing." He snapped his fingers. "That woman cares. A lot more than she's let on. And not just for Maura, either."

He was inordinately pleased with the knowledge that Catherine didn't want anybody's baby but his. He drummed his fingers on the steering wheel. Why did it matter so much? Damn, but he was stupid. He cared because Catherine had very sneakily wormed her way into his heart. It hurt that Catherine had given up her dreams. Because of him. For him.

"Stupid," he muttered. "Really stupid." Well, he wasn't going to let her get away with it. He'd see to it her every dream was fulfilled, or happily die in bed trying, and that was that. Jason picked up his car phone and made a phone call, then pulled into traffic and headed home.

Maura was already home when he got there. He fed her dinner, then packed her back into the car and dropped her off at Monica's. He then picked up the crib Monica had had her pregnant neighbor buy at Hand Arounds after Jason's earlier phone call.

"Jane said Catherine got all misty-eyed when she loaded it into her car," Monica reported as she helped Jason.

"Yeah, well, I'm going to take care of that," Jason promised. "She'll never get misty-eyed again, not if I can help it."

Monica stopped and stared at him in amazement. "Don't be stupid!" she said.

Jason slammed the car door and turned to her. "What?"

"Jason, she's probably going to cry all over you when she sees what you've got. Heck, I'm getting all teary-eyed right now just thinking about how romantic this all is."

"Don't you dare start weeping," Jason said in a threatening voice. "Don't you dare." He sighed. "What is it with you women, crying over every little thing? This isn't that big a deal. I'm just going to marry her and get her pregnant, that's all. Get a grip, Monica." He reached into the front seat. "Here. Maura forgot to take her flute in, accidentally on purpose, I'm sure. Make her practice. I'll be back as soon as I drop this off and talk some sense into that sister of yours." With that he climbed into his car and backed down Monica's driveway.

Ten minutes later he rang Catherine's doorbell.

"Hi," he said when she answered. "It's me. I need to talk to you."

Catherine looked around for Maura and was disappointed not to see her. She'd felt awkward around Jason ever since Christmas, and Maura provided a nice buffer. "Uh, sure. Okay, I guess. Come on in."

"I've got some stuff to bring in first. Hold the door open so I can get this in."

Catherine blinked. "What?" She looked around to the side of the house next to the door. There was a crib and mattress leaning there. She looked harder. *Her* crib and mattress. "I sold that today," she informed him blankly.

"Yeah. To somebody who was getting it for me." He picked up the mattress which wobbled all over the place as he tried to angle it through the doorway. "Watch out. I don't want to knock you down."

"Jason—"

"No, Catherine, just listen. I can't let you give up on your dream, you hear me? You were made for loving. Both the giving and the getting kind. You're putting this thing back up in that bedroom, and I'll help you fill it as many times as you want to. But, the deal is, you're going to have to marry me first."

Catherine's mouth gaped open. "Excuse me?"

"You heard me. And I don't want any of your grief over this, either. No, you'll just have to be reasonable and let me give you a baby. I love you too much not to."

"No, you don't," she argued, stunned by the sudden declaration. "I'm the one who loves you."

"Yeah," he agreed. "I finally figured that part out,

but it's only half the equation. Turn the light on in the upstairs hall, would you? I can't see a thing."

Catherine hastened after him up the stairs. "Jason stop. I don't understand what's happening. What's this all about?"

"Can't stop. This thing's awkward as hell." But when he reached the second floor, he leaned the mattress against the wall and turned to pull her into his embrace. He kissed her. She sagged against him. "This is what it's all about, Cath. I love you, you love me. We're going to get married and make beautiful babies together. Simple. What's so hard to grasp about it?"

Jason was holding her up with an arm around her waist. Good thing, too. Otherwise she'd have fallen. "You're insane," she said against his chest, and tried to remember how to breathe.

"No, I've never been saner. I've finally got it all straight in my head, Cath, and I'm sorry as can be for how long it took me. You must have gone through hell selling your crib. It represented everything you've ever wanted, didn't it?" He picked up the mattress and continued down the hall. "The ring's in my back pocket," he informed her. "I was too embarrassed to return it to the store after Christmas. I'll give it to you as soon as I get the rest of the crib back up here. You got a screwdriver? I'll put it together again for you."

Catherine scurried after him. "Jason, wait. This is all so sudden. What about you? You didn't want a baby. You even said so. I can't let you do this."

He shuffled the mattress into the nursery and let it fall onto the floor. Then he grabbed her and kissed her again, this time slipping his tongue past her lips and wreaking total havoc in her mouth and all through her body. Catherine actually slipped to her knees before he caught her again when he was done.

He smiled in a superior, male sort of fashion. "Like you'd almost be able to stop me if I put my mind to it," he said smugly. He guided her over to the crib mattress and let her sit down there. "I've got to bring in the rest of the bed," he said, looking down at her. "Wait here. I'll be right back." He turned, started out of the room.

Catherine lifted her arm to his retreating figure. "Wait. Jason, look, I—"

He turned back, came to tower over her. "No, you look." He dropped to his knees beside her. "I know I'm not handling this well. It's been a rough afternoon. Heavy-duty personal insights can do that to you." Jason ran a hand through his hair, then caught up her hands in his. "Okay, romance. That's why you're reluctant, right? This isn't romantic enough. Let me think for a minute." He shuffled forward on his knees. He looked her right in the eye. "Catherine, I love you. I probably have for a long time, only I'm a little slow and just figured it out this afternoon. I need you in my life. Not to help me understand Maura's adolescence, although I won't deny that's an added bonus, but for me. *I* need you. You're my joy, my sunshine, and I've never been so scared or so bummed as when I saw that crib in your shop window. It hit me like a kick in the gut. Don't ever do anything like that again."

"Oh, Jason—"

He kissed her quiet. She collapsed on the carpet.

Jason followed her down. "There's nothing I want more than to make babies with you," he told her, placing damp kisses all over her face and neck. "Nothing."

Jason slid his hand up under her sweater and filled his palm with her breast. Her breath hitched, and she wrapped her arms around his neck. "Jason, are you sure?"

He came over her and nestled his lower body into the warmth between her legs. "Does that feel like I have any doubts on the matter?"

No. No, it didn't. His arousal was hard and substantial against her. He was also working her sweater off her in a rather determined fashion. "Oh, Jason, I love you so much," Catherine whispered as her head briefly disappeared into the soft wool of her top.

"I know, baby. I love you, too. Catherine?"

"Yes?"

"Is this the bra you paid $28 for?"

"No. It's a new one. It cost $35."

Jason's eyes crossed. "Oh, God, I'm a dead man."

Over the next eight years, Jason and Catherine filled the cradle three times. Then Maura took it over. She filled it twice. Their son and his wife used it, and their two daughters, as well.

That crib, the fake heirloom, became a real one. By the time Maura's oldest child took it home with her, she considered it an honest-to-goodness real and precious heirloom, the only bed she wanted her baby to sleep in.

*   *   *   *   *

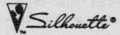
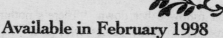

Take 4 bestselling love stories FREE

Plus get a FREE surprise gift!

Special Limited-time Offer

Mail to Silhouette Reader Service™

3010 Walden Avenue
P.O. Box 1867
Buffalo, N.Y. 14240-1867

YES! Please send me 4 free Silhouette Romance™ novels and my free surprise gift. Then send me 6 brand-new novels every month, which I will receive months before they appear in bookstores. Bill me at the low price of $2.67 each plus 25¢ delivery and applicable sales tax, if any.* That's the complete price and a savings of over 10% off the cover prices—quite a bargain! I understand that accepting the books and gift places me under no obligation ever to buy any books. I can always return a shipment and cancel at any time. Even if I never buy another book from Silhouette, the 4 free books and the surprise gift are mine to keep forever.

215 BPA A3UT

Name	(PLEASE PRINT)	
Address	Apt. No.	
City	State	Zip

This offer is limited to one order per household and not valid to present Silhouette Romance™ subscribers. *Terms and prices are subject to change without notice. Sales tax applicable in N.Y.

USROM-696 ©1990 Harlequin Enterprises Limited

Return to the Towers!

In March
New York Times bestselling author

NORA ROBERTS

brings us to the Calhouns' fabulous
Maine coast mansion and reveals the
tragic secrets hidden there for generations.

For all his degrees, Professor Max Quartermain has a
lot to learn about love—and luscious Lilah Calhoun is
just the woman to teach him. Ex-cop Holt Bradford is
as prickly as a thornbush—until Suzanna Calhoun's
special touch makes love blossom in his heart.
And all of them are caught in the race to solve
the generations-old mystery of a priceless
lost necklace...and a timeless love.

Lilah and Suzanna
THE
Calhoun Women

**A special 2-in-1 edition containing
FOR THE LOVE OF LILAH and
SUZANNA'S SURRENDER**

Available at your favorite retail outlet.

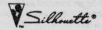

He's more than a man, he's one of our

Fabulous Fathers

Join Silhouette Romance as we present these
heartwarming tales about wonderful men facing
the challenges of fatherhood and love.

January 1998:
THE BILLIONAIRE'S BABY CHASE by Valerie Parv (SR#1270)
Billionaire daddy James Langford finds himself falling for Zoe Holden, the
alluring foster mother of his long-lost daughter.

March 1998:
IN CARE OF THE SHERIFF by Susan Meier (SR#1283)
Sexy sheriff Ryan Kelly becomes a father-in-training when he is stranded
with beautiful Madison Delaney and her adorable baby.

May 1998:
FALLING FOR A FATHER OF FOUR by Arlene James (SR#1295)
Overwhelmed single father Orren Ellis is soon humming the wedding march
after hiring new nanny Mattie Kincaid.

Fall in love with our FABULOUS FATHERS!

And be sure to look for additional FABULOUS FATHERS titles
in the months to come.

Available at your favorite retail outlet.

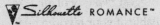

Silhouette ROMANCE™

Look us up on-line at: http://www.romance.net   SRFFJ-M

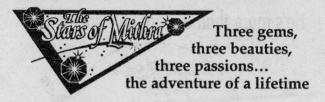

The Stars of Mithra

**Three gems,
three beauties,
three passions...
the adventure of a lifetime**

SILHOUETTE·INTIMATE·MOMENTS®
brings you a thrilling new series by
New York Times bestselling author

Nora Roberts

**Three mystical blue diamonds place three close
friends in jeopardy...and lead them to romance.**

In October
HIDDEN STAR (IM#811)
Bailey James can't remember a thing, but she knows
she's in big trouble. And she desperately needs private
investigator Cade Parris to help her live long enough to
find out just what kind.

In December
CAPTIVE STAR (IM#823)
Cynical bounty hunter Jack Dakota and spitfire
M. J. O'Leary are handcuffed together and on the run
from a pair of hired killers. And Jack wants to know
why—but M.J.'s not talking.

In February
SECRET STAR (IM#835)
Lieutenant Seth Buchanan's murder investigation takes
a strange turn when Grace Fontaine turns up alive. But
as the mystery unfolds, he soon discovers the notorious
heiress is the biggest mystery of all.

Available at your favorite retail outlet.

SUSAN MALLERY

Continues the twelve-book series—36 HOURS—in January 1998 with Book Seven

THE RANCHER AND THE RUNAWAY BRIDE

When Randi Howell fled the altar, she'd been running for her life! And she'd kept on running—straight into the arms of rugged rancher Brady Jones. She knew he had his suspicions, but how could she tell him the truth about her identity? Then again, if she ever wanted to approach the altar in earnest, how could she not?

For Brady and Randi and *all* the residents of Grand Springs, Colorado, the storm-induced blackout was just the beginning of 36 Hours that changed *everything!* You won't want to miss a single book.

Available at your favorite retail outlet.

Look us up on-line at: http://www.romance.net

36HRS7

Welcome to the Towers!

In January
New York Times bestselling author

NORA ROBERTS

takes us to the fabulous Maine coast mansion
haunted by a generations-old secret and introduces
us to the fascinating family that lives there.

Mechanic Catherine "C.C." Calhoun and hotel magnate
Trenton St. James mix like axle grease and mineral
water—until they kiss. Efficient Amanda Calhoun finds
easygoing Sloan O'Riley insufferable—and irresistible.
And they all must race to solve the mystery
surrounding a priceless hidden emerald necklace.

Catherine and Amanda

THE Calhoun Women

**A special 2-in-1 edition containing
COURTING CATHERINE and A MAN FOR AMANDA.**

Look for the next installment of
THE CALHOUN WOMEN with Lilah and Suzanna's
stories, coming in March 1998.

Available at your favorite retail outlet.